ON THE RUN

William must have known that it was useless—that I couldn't go on. "I'll lead them off to the left," he said. "The first chance you get, leave the path and hide."

We ran a few more yards, and when I saw my opportunity I veered off the path. The sound of William's footfalls moved farther and farther away from me. Then I heard voices.

"I think she's over here, on the right," a man said.

I heard a noise and knew at once what it was. The men had left the path and were coming through the brush in my direction. I did the only thing I could. I dropped down to the ground and crawled inside a hollow log. I lay motionless, listening and waiting. Trembling and praying . . . as I heard the men approaching the log.

ECHOES
IN THE
GROVE

PATRICIA SIERRA

AN AVON FLARE BOOK

ECHOES IN THE GROVE is an original publication of Avon Books. This work has never before appeared in book form. This work is a novel. Any similarity to actual persons or events is purely coincidental.

AVON BOOKS
A division of
The Hearst Corporation
1350 Avenue of the Americas
New York, New York 10019

Copyright © 1994 by Patricia Sierra
Published by arrangement with the author
Library of Congress Catalog Card Number: 93-91017
ISBN: 0-380-76940-9
RL: 5.8

First Avon Flare Printing: July 1994

AVON FLARE TRADEMARK REG. U.S. PAT. OFF. AND IN OTHER COUNTRIES, MARCA REGISTRADA, HECHO EN U.S.A.

Printed in the U.S.A.

RA   10   9   8   7   6   5   4   3   2   1

For Stephanie, Stacie, and Sandor Frank

Although *Echoes in the Grove* is a work of fiction, many of the events described and the people portrayed are based on information found in a variety of published local histories. My debt is greatest to *The Pioneer Scrap-Book of Wood County and the Maumee Valley,* gathered from the papers and manuscripts of C. W. Evers (Bowling Green, Ohio, 1909), and *The East Side: Past and Present* by Isaac Wright (Hadley & Hadley, Toledo, Ohio, 1894).

One

July 1854

The night was quiet, except for a choir of locusts, and hotter than usual for July in Ohio. I think I was awake, but may have been only dreaming that I was, when a single, anguished howl pierced the dark—a sound so primitive, it seemed almost animal. Frightened, I rushed to my parents' bed.

Mother asked Father what could have made such an awful sound. He said he didn't know, but he was certain that it came from the direction of the Pecks' farm, a quarter mile away.

"You must go there," she said.

"No, Hannah," he told her.

We lived in a swampy portion of the forest where, even in daylight, walking was precarious. I suspected that Father had no enthusiasm for setting out on foot so soon after a lengthy rain.

"But there could be trouble at the Pecks'," Mother insisted.

"Well, whatever it was is over now," Father assured her. And he was right. We all three held our breath, listening. The only sound was a distant owl.

1

I was still kindling up the fire for breakfast when Father took down his gun from the pegs by the door. "Sit yourself down, John. You need something in your stomach. You haven't even had your coffee," Mother said.

"I want to take a look at the Pecks' place first."

"Then I am going with you." She untied her apron as she spoke.

"Me, too," I said.

They exchanged a look but didn't say no. I buttoned my shoes as fast as I could, but by the time I finished, they were already pushing their way into the cornfield that marks the end of our land and the beginning of the Pecks' farm. I had to run to catch up.

When we reached the old log cabin that was the Pecks' house, Father put out his arm, blocking Mother and me from the door. "Stand back there, by the apple tree," he said. We did as we were told.

Father held his gun steady with both hands, ready to shoot. Using the toe of his boot, he tapped the weathered door three times. When no one responded, he lifted the latch—slowly, quietly—and pushed the door ajar. At first, he stood as still as a statue. He seemed to be listening as intently as he does when in the forest, stalking deer. Then, just a few heartbeats later, he returned to the tree where Mother and I waited.

"I hear a noise inside," he told us.

"What is it?" Mother asked.

"I don't know. It's a snapping, breaking sound."

"I think we should go in," she said.

Before answering, Father looked toward the house then back at us. "No," he said. "I want both of you to stay here."

2

He returned to the unlatched door and, with the barrel of his gun, coaxed it open a little farther. He took half a step inside, then stopped. His back tensed, telling us something was wrong. We inched toward him, afraid.

Father turned toward us. "You'd better go inside," he said, "and see if you can help." I knew he was speaking to Mother, but when he stepped aside, allowing her to enter the cabin, I followed.

What we found was a forlorn-looking Mrs. Peck, sitting in a ladder-back chair, cracking walnuts. Her husband lay dead on the floor beside her.

"He took ill last night," Mrs. Peck explained, though not necessarily to us. She didn't seem to know we were there. "I gave him a dose of turpentine, but it didn't help."

Mrs. Peck glanced up and noticed Mother. She leaned toward her, whispering, "I think Thomas is very sick."

"Yes," Mother whispered. She knelt down and took Mrs. Peck's hand. "Why don't you come home with us and have some breakfast?"

Mrs. Peck shook her head. "I can't leave Thomas. I told you he's very sick. And I don't feel so well myself."

Mother led Father and me outdoors. She told me to go home and attend to the chores. Then she turned to Father and said, "I will stay here—to wash Thomas and put him in his suit. You gather the neighbors. Tell them we have someone to send home to Jesus. There's a coffin to build, a grave to dig. . . ."

At least two hours passed before Father and the other men returned to the Pecks' farm. By then, Mrs. Peck lay on her bed, chilled and feverish. Mother sat with her until she died.

3

A few hours later, Mother was stricken.

For a long time afterward, I wasn't able to say that my mother was dead. Not aloud.

It seemed an insult to her that she should die at a time of so many losses. Day after day, neighbors from one edge of the woods to the other had risen for breakfast, just like always, only to die before midnight. Mother's departure was just one more—just another name added to a list that grew by the hour. Grief for her was mingled with grief for dozens of others. All the dead were stirred together until their individual identities merged into one, like flavors in a soup.

A few days after the dying began, two men stopped to ask if either Father or I had fallen ill and needed help. One said there was talk that the sickness, the cholera, had arrived on a boat from Buffalo. When the sailors came ashore, they brought it with them, into our shops and taverns. From there, it traveled home on the cuffs of trousers and the hems of skirts. Soon it was everywhere, in coffeepots and cradles, on the tines of forks and the pages of books. It pushed outward from the heart of the city, across the fields and into the forests, touching all in its path—killing the weak and weakening the strong.

"People are packing everything they can," one man said. "When they run out of trunks, they start filling hatboxes, tool bins, and feed bags."

"That's right," his companion agreed. "On all the main roads, overloaded wagons are strung as close as pearls. Half are stuck in the mud. A man with a broken leg could walk faster than they're riding."

The men said they had heard some of the runaways begging Dr. Simon to come with them. The epidemic was too big to stop, they told him. He'd end up as dead as all the others if he stayed. But Dr. Simon wouldn't leave, even though (or, perhaps, *because)* his own wife and son were among the first to die. He owned the only drugstore in our corner of the county. The door was left open at all times so the sick could help themselves to the medicines he prescribed.

Dr. Simon was so deprived of sleep, a contingent of neighbors finally resorted to blocking his path as he attempted to exit his house. They insisted that he stay in for one full night so that he might rest and prepare for the strains of the coming day. The largest, strongest men stood guard at his door—keeping patients out and Dr. Simon in.

After Mother died, Father did not stay home to nurse his grief. That would have been too big a luxury at a time of so much need. He went into town to help Seth Byer build coffins. Others were helping, too—night and day. When there was no longer enough room in Seth's cabinet shop for all the volunteers, the large central hall of the courthouse was turned into a workshop.

In the beginning, no one was buried without a coffin. But then the demand for Seth's pine boxes grew far faster than he and his crew could nail the planks together. More than a hundred of our loved ones had perished in less than a month. Tom Sheehan lost his wife and all five of his children.

One of the first of Seth's coffins was made for Mother. Because it was built early, when the deaths were fewer and the time between them longer, the workmanship was admirable. I could rub my hand over every surface without collecting splinters, and each of the corners met in perfect points. But before even a week had passed, any board would do, even those with knotholes.

This troubled Father. I knew because I had read what he wrote in a letter to Mother's sister, my aunt Sarah:

All Seth's helpers mean well. But from the way they so eagerly reach for whatever's at hand—wormy wood, rusty nails—it is clear they've forgotten what precious cargo these boxes carry. When I asked Seth to construct a coffin for Hannah, I told him to infuse it with as much tenderness and as much love as that other carpenter, Jesus, would.

We lived in a house hewn from the timber of our own trees. I slept in a loft above the main room where we cooked and ate our meals. The two chairs closest to the hearth were large and cushioned, with footstools to match.

From my bed, I often eavesdropped on my parents as they sat in those chairs, enjoying the warmth of the fire at night. Long after they thought I was safely asleep, they would tell each other things they would never say to me. The winter before she died, Mother spoke of a quilt she intended to sew. "It will have squares from my wedding dress, Rebecca's first blanket, your pale blue shirt," she said. "Snippets of memories from all of us—my sisters and yours, aunts we almost never see, uncles whose names we barely know. . . . I've been saving them since I was a little girl. It will be the most beautiful quilt in Ohio. You'll see."

"But we have plenty of covers," Father said.

"You don't understand. It won't be just a cover. It will be art."

"Like a painting?" he asked.

"Yes, like a painting," she said.

My first blanket would have been fourteen years old by then. Nearly fifteen. It pleased me to know that Mother had saved a part of it. But I was surprised by her plan to make a quilt. Her mind seemed too crowded with the business of preparing custards and eliminating cobwebs to allow much room for needless needlework. Soon after I overheard the conversation about the quilt, I asked if she'd teach me the stitches a girl must know to sew a proper sampler.

"Not until our chores are done," she said—and, of course, they never were.

I will always wish that I had learned those stitches in time.

Friends warned us that Mother was contagious. "She should be put in the ground at once," they said. Muscled men from miles around offered to help, but Father insisted on digging her grave himself. He chose a plot in the grove, just below the hill where our house sits. It's the only place in that small stand of trees where the overhead branches separate, allowing sunlight to reach the ground. It is there that the snow first begins to melt each spring.

Night fell before the ground was ready. I knew that Father would wait until morning to bury her. The only thing she ever feared was the dark.

He placed the coffin in a circle of moonlight, near the grave, and removed the lid. Then he sat down beside Mother and remained there through the night, except for a few moments when he returned to the

7

house. From my perch in the loft, I watched as he moved quietly across the large room below me.

He went to the blanket box where Mother stored the embroidered pillow that was given to them on their wedding day. She said it was too pretty to use; it was reserved for guests who stayed the night, though none ever did. Father didn't know I was watching when he opened the box and took out the pillow.

When he went outside again, I crept down the ladder to the main room—avoiding the rung that squeaks—and slipped out into the dark, following Father to the grove. We were dangerously close, but I kept well hidden in the shadows of the trees. I had learned stealthiness from Father. He was a tracker and trapper by trade, two skills he taught me early.

From behind the veil of a weeping willow, I watched as Father returned to the circle of moonlight where Mother lay. I saw how gently he placed the embroidered pillow under her head and how tenderly he kissed her goodnight for the last time.

Although Reverend Markin had told us that Heaven was perfect, I knew Father believed—as I did—that Mother's arrival immediately improved it.

Two

As the cholera subsided, settlements on both sides of the river were visited by a different, yet similar, sickness—the ague, a malady that arrives and departs with the mosquitoes each summer. Like cholera, the ague brings on fever, chills, and a quaking of the body so strong, it has been said to cause a house to tremble. But unlike cholera, it is seldom fatal. The patient suffers alternating days of prostrate illness and halfhearted healthiness until, at last, the frost comes and the mosquitoes leave.

When Father came down with the ague, I feared at first that it was cholera and he would die. He shared that fear.

"Bring me some paper and a pencil," he said, barely able to lift himself from his pillow.

Because I knew he would be embarrassed by the tremor of his hand, I offered to write down whatever he said.

"Yes," he agreed, settling back on his bed, "that would be good. This is a letter to your aunt Sarah. Begin it 'My dear Sarah.'"

My dear Sarah, I wrote.

"I am writing to you today to state in clear terms

my desire that the care and custody of Rebecca be consigned to you in the event of my death."

My heart stopped.

"Write it, Rebecca."

I looked down at the pencil, but could not will my hand to move it. "I . . ."

"Please, Rebecca."

"I'm sorry, but I can't." I put the paper and pencil on the bed beside him, excused myself, and went outdoors. Father called after me, but I pretended not to hear.

The afternoon air felt heavy with humidity and so thick I was certain I could see it. A fat mosquito appeared ready to dine on my arm, reminding me it was time to prepare the smudge pots—our only weapon against the armies of mosquitoes that invaded our swampy forest each evening from July to September.

I poured oil into two pots, then held a piece of kindling in the outside fire where we did our summer cooking. When it caught the flame, I transferred the fire to the smudge pots and watched the dense, black smoke begin to billow. I put one pot in the barn with Victoria, our cow, and the other in the house with Father.

I told Father I would have to use our tablecloth to cover Victoria. "The files and mosquitoes are chewing her raw," I said. I didn't know whether he was asleep or just too weak to argue.

I opened the cupboard where the tablecloth was kept, not expecting to feel as I did when I saw it. Mother had made it from a length of yellow fabric sold to her by an Indian woman who often stopped at our house, selling her weavings. "It's for our Christmas table," Mother told us, beaming. She had every right to be proud. With a sprig of holly embroidered

10

in each of the four corners, it was the most beautiful thing she had ever sewn.

I meant to reach for the tablecloth, but the sight of it stopped me, flooding my heart with memories of Mother. There must be something else large enough to cover Victoria, I thought.

Our blankets were exempt (Father and I needed them to hide under when the mosquitoes attacked at night), and the cleaning rags were too small—so I thought of the box under my parents' bed, the one where Mother stored her needles, thread, and fabric.

I crept toward the bed, trying not to disturb Father. I could see the box precisely where I remembered it to be. By getting down on my hands and knees, I was able to reach it and, with some effort, pull it toward me, out into the room. It was surprisingly heavy. When I lifted the lid, I saw why. The box was brimming with spools of thread, yards of cotton and wool—and the neatly cut fragments Mother had been saving for her quilt. I recognized the square on top: it was cut from the white curtains that used to hang in the window in the loft. At the center of the square was an embroidered flower—an Indian pipe that looked as fresh and real as any in a vase.

Beneath that square was another, this one cut from Mother's apron—and there, too, was an embroidered flower (this time, an exquisite lilac). I hurried through the stacks of squares, looking at the garden Mother had grown—roses, daises, lilies, forget-me-nots, all perfectly rendered with thread and needle— hours of work that I had never seen her perform. I remembered her words to Father. Her quilt would be a piece of art, she had said, but to my eyes it already was. Even unassembled, it could have caused any ribbon-winning quilt at the County Fair to blush with

11

shame. I wondered when all that beauty had been made. It couldn't have been during the day. Cooking, cleaning, fetching water, milking the cow—there was far too much of real life demanding Mother's time and attention to allow room for such painstaking stitchery. I thought of the many nights when I had awakened, but only partly, to a noise or movement in the room below. Reassured by the glow of the lamp, I would drift back to sleep. Father used to complain of Mother's relentless wanderings in the night, but now I suspected that she had roamed no farther than her needle.

My first impulse was to awaken Father and show him my discovery, but almost at once I decided against it. I thought it might make him sadder, if that was possible. His face had grown so long and lined since Mother died, I found myself avoiding all mention of her. I was waiting for *him* to say her name, to show me that it was safe. But as the days rolled into weeks, it seemed that such a time might never come.

I removed the largest piece of cloth from the box but left the embroidered squares just as I had found them, in tidy stacks. After securing the lid, I pushed the box back under Father's bed.

Unfolded, the cloth proved to be more than ample to cover Victoria. I took it out to the well, where I saturated it with water, hoping that would make it cling to Victoria's hide. Then I carried it, dripping, to the barn. I was so intent on keeping my dress dry, I didn't notice that someone had ridden up on horseback.

Ashley Bissell was the silver-haired banker who took my aunt Sarah to be his wife soon after he first spied her working in his neighbor's home. She had moved into town to keep house for the Motts in exchange for room, board, and both the time and tuition needed to attend the high school. After graduation, Aunt Sarah stayed on with the Motts, preferring to continue her employment rather than returning to her parents' cabin and plot of land, where she would be expected to help with the planting and harvesting each year. She didn't look forward to the hard work of trying to grow corn where a swamp used to be.

Uncle Ash, a widower, asked Aunt Sarah to marry him, even though his children were older than she and did not accept the union. Aunt Sarah said yes for a reason that surprised everyone but herself and Uncle Ash: she loved him, truly loved him.

Of all the people in the world, Uncle Ash was the last one I would have expected to see smiling down at me from his horse that late summer day. He was a gentleman—never without a shine on his shoes or a solid gold watch in his fob. From visits at his house, I had carried home memories of a man accustomed to meticulous tailoring. It surprised me that he would put his wardrobe at such great risk by riding out to our house, through the remnants of the Black Swamp, knowing that he and his horse might have been swallowed by the ground at any moment. On the main road, taverns with sleeping quarters were seldom more than a mile apart—ready to provide rest and restoration to unfortunate travelers whose wagons sank wheel-deep in the mud. In one day's time, some wagons moved no more than half a mile, giving the occupants a choice of lodgings for the night: the tavern half a mile back, or the one half a mile ahead. On horseback, a traveler might have advanced faster, with less chance of sinking, but not without splatters on his clothes. I knew that Uncle Ash had not come to see us about a trivial matter.

"Uncle Ash!" I exclaimed. I was happy to see him, and I knew it showed.

"Hello, Rebecca," he said with a broad smile.

"I can't believe you're really here."

He dismounted and tied his horse to the post by the barn. I hurried into his waiting hug.

"Sarah sent me to talk to you and your father."

I could tell from his voice that he had come on a serious mission.

"What is it, Uncle Ash?"

"Let's find your Father."

"He's sick with the ague. I think he's sleeping."

"Then boil me a big cup of coffee and tell me . . ." His voice trailed off into silence.

"It's all right," I told him. "You can say it. You want to know how we're getting along without Mother."

He looked relieved. "Yes."

"It isn't easy," I said. "When she died, Father went away, too. He sits across the table from me at every meal, but he isn't there. Not truly. Not since the day he buried Mother."

I walked as I spoke, leading Uncle Ash to the outdoor fire where we did our summer cooking. After feeding more kindling to the embers, I filled our granite pot with a mixture of water and freshly ground coffee, then placed it on the metal grate that stood on steel legs above the flames.

"What about *you?*" Uncle Ash asked.

"I can't quite believe that Mother is dead. Absorbing a thought as large as that is difficult. It takes time."

I walked with Uncle Ash to the edge of the hill to

show him where Mother was buried. "She's down there," I said, pointing to a small grassy mound in the grove.

Uncle Ash started down the hill, but I held back.

"Come with me," he said, but it was more a question than an order.

"I'm afraid I'll disappear if I do."

"Disappear?"

"Yes, disappear and never come back—just like Mother . . . and the Indian. . . ."

"What do you mean?"

"An Indian woman who sells her weavings to families along the river came here one day when I was hanging the clothes to dry. Her English was good. She told me she knew something sad about our home."

"Did she tell you what it was?"

"Yes."

"And did she tell you how she knew it?"

"She said she knew it from a legend. When she told me the story, I listened with interest but soon forgot it. Then Mother died, and now I think of it every day."

Uncle Ash sat down in the grass. He patted the ground. "Come, sit down here. Tell me the story."

I hesitated. "You'll think I'm foolish."

"I won't. I promise."

"We need two things first," I said, slapping at the mosquitoes. "A smudge pot and coffee."

I went into the house to get a mug from the cupboard, moving quietly so as not to disturb Father. When I stepped back outside, I saw that Uncle Ash had prepared the smudge pot. I filled the mug with steaming coffee and carried it to the edge of the hill where he sat waiting for me in a waft of black

15

smoke. He didn't speak until I was settled on the ground beside him.

"Now," he said, leaning slightly toward me, "tell me about the Indian legend."

A Shawnee brave had dared to fall in love with Shut-nok, the beautiful, dark-eyed daughter of Chief Tondoganie. But the chief was quick to forbid the young lovers to see each other. Although the brave was of noble birth, his tribe was small. Chief Tondoganie could not approve a suitor of such low station.

The brave lived many miles away but made frequent trips to the river under the pretext of fishing when, in fact, he was meeting in secret with Shut-nok. Chief Tondoganie was not deceived. He confronted the brave, ordering him to go away and never return.

The brave knew that the penalty of disobedience would be death. With a broken heart, he returned to his home in the plains. But Shut-nok could not let go so easily. She followed her handsome brave to the top of a hill that looked out over a grove. From there, she watched as he walked farther and farther away from her, down the hill and through the grove, disappearing completely and forever into the distance.

Shut-nok returned to her father, but her mood was dark ever after. She would slip away for whole days and nights at a time, causing her father great worry. Invariably, he sent his runners looking for her, and, invariably, they came back with this story: Shut-nok had been traced to the top of a hill—where she stood, a lone silhouette against the sky, chanting a mournful song.

One day Shut-nok left her father's wigwam and never returned. But for years afterward, people reported seeing an Indian girl standing on the peak of a hill in the dark of night. And they claimed that a strange, haunting song—a funeral dirge—could be heard echoing in the grove below.

"I asked the Indian woman if she was certain that it was *our* hill, *our* grove. She told me to listen some night when the world feels empty. I would hear the song then, she said."

"And did you?" Uncle Ash asked.

"I've heard it every night since Mother died."

"Your mind is too idle, Rebecca."

"Idle? I am busy from the time I climb out of my bed in the morning until I lay myself back down at night."

"Your hands may be busy, but your mind is idle—too vulnerable to the influence of Indian tales."

I felt myself blushing. "I knew you would think that I was foolish."

"That's not what I think at all. I think you need to pick up your life where it left off in July."

That sounded wonderful to me. More than anything else I could imagine, I wanted my life to be exactly as it used to be—before Mother took sick, before I put on her apron as if it were my own, before I embarked on her unfinished tasks as if they mattered. It was good that my thoughts were silent. If Father could have heard what my heart and my mind sometimes whispered to each other, it would have been a powerful disappointment to him. He would have thought that I didn't wish to help with the work. But he would have been wrong. I did want to help. I

17

just didn't like feeling that I'd handed my entire life over to a house, a barn, and a cow. What I missed most, besides Mother, was a quiet hour now and then when, without guilt, I could set down my kettle and pick up a book.

"Your aunt Sarah has sent me here to invite you to live in our house during the school term," Uncle Ash said.

I never realized how much I had loved school until it was denied me. For two months of every year—the mosquitoless, blizzardless months of September and October—classes were held in a one-room structure just a mile from our house. But after the cholera claimed our teacher, Mrs. Hatcher, there was neither the money nor the interest to hire a replacement. Mrs. Hatcher always smelled of cinnamon, as if she had just come from her kitchen. I missed her. And I missed the huge dictionary that sat, open, on a book stand near my desk. I loved to search its pages for new words that I could make mine forever simply by learning them. Mrs. Hatcher said that my spelling was the best of all the students she had ever taught. Saying the letters of a word made me feel powerful— like a mason cementing bricks, building something substantial and whole.

"I do wish I were in school," I admitted. I especially wished that I were enrolled in the tall, brick school that Uncle Ash was inviting me to attend. It was located in town, near Aunt Sarah's house, holding classes for ten months (not just two) each year. The curriculum was challenging—far more so than any our humble, rural school had ever offered. Some of the teachers had even been to college.

"Good," Uncle Ash said. "I'll tell Sarah that you're coming."

"But I can't just leave. There's work to be done. Father would miss me."

Uncle Ash nodded his head. "We want your father to come, too."

"Father would never agree to live in town. He would feel as if he were caught in one of his own traps."

"It won't be forever. Just for the school term."

"I know he won't go. And he won't let me go, either."

"We'll see," Uncle Ash said.

He stood up and walked toward the house.

"Are you going to ask him now?"

"Yes."

"Do you think you should wake him?"

Uncle Ash stopped. "Do you think I shouldn't?"

I thought for a moment. Maybe Father *would* let me go to Aunt Sarah's. Maybe.

Uncle Ash didn't wait for my answer. He continued toward the house.

Three

When Uncle Ash stepped from the house, he appeared so self-satisfied, I knew at once he had negotiated an agreement with Father.

"I will send a carriage for you on Saturday," he said.

"Just me?"

"Your Father and I reached a compromise. You both will come to our house on Saturday. He will stay until he is well enough to resume his work. You will remain through the school year."

I looked past Uncle Ash, toward the house.

"He says he will visit," Uncle Ash assured me. When I didn't respond, he added, "Frequently."

I knew that was true. Father made regular trips into town to sell the pelts of the animals he trapped. I knew that I might even see him as often as I would have had I remained at the cabin. His work required him to leave home for days at a time when he hunted bears and deer. But even so, I was at war with myself—excited at the prospect of attending such an excellent school, surrounded by others my age, yet guilty to be abandoning Father. At least he would be coming to Aunt Sarah's for a while. If it proved to be the nurturing haven I expected it to be, perhaps he would stay ... perhaps he would finally return from that distant place where he had taken the warmth and humor that used to spill from him.

Saturday dawned after three days of sunshine that left the land firmer, less muddy than usual. Father took the reins from Horace, the driver Uncle Ash sent to fetch us, preferring to direct the carriage himself. Few men knew the forest as Father did, off road and on. He had tracked both man and animal in sunlight and moonlight, every season of the year. He knew where the ground was apt to dip, where the wagon was prone to sink. He propelled us with such skill and efficiency, we arrived at Aunt Sarah's in time for an early dinner.

Horace helped us with our belongings, leaving only the smaller satchels for us to carry up the front steps, across the porch, and into the wide central hall—the heart of the house from which all the first-floor rooms flowed. Here, too, was where the carpeted stairway began its elegant climb upward.

I heard Aunt Sarah's approach moments before I could see her. The rustle of her petticoats, the music of her voice wrapped 'round me like a mother's embrace. She began saying, "Hello, hello, hello," a full room away, rushing toward us as if it had been years rather than months since she had seen us. She hugged me before I could even reach toward her, telling me how happy, how delighted, how ecstatic she was to see me and Father, too, of course.

I stepped back to look at that face I loved so much. Aunt Sarah looked truly beautiful—with flawless skin, enormous green eyes, and copper-colored curls.

Her figure was slight, yet nicely curved, and in no way bony.

"Look how grown-up you are," she said, appraising me from head to toe. She turned to Father and whispered, "She's the image of Hannah."

He nodded, and that disturbed me. I had no wish to be his daily reminder of Mother, no matter how complimented I was by the resemblance.

While Horace carried our belongings upstairs, Aunt Sarah led us into the dining room, where a lunch of pork, baked apples, and warm bread awaited us. Her table was set with hand-painted china, crystal goblets, and polished silver utensils atop a delicate lace cloth. Uncle Ash sat at the south end of the table, as straight as a pillar in his fine dark suit and silken ascot.

Seeing Father in such a setting was like finding a burr in a jewelry box, but Aunt Sarah chirped at him all through the meal, never once seeming to notice his country clothes and dusty manners. To me, he was a mirror, revealing my own shortcomings. I was ashamed of neither of us; only concerned that we might, during our stay, cause embarrassment for our relatives. Thus I was relieved when, after lunch, I overheard Aunt Sarah instruct Mary, her servant girl, to take the clothing from our baggage and use it as patterns for my new dresses and Father's new trousers and shirts.

"Trousers?" Father boomed. "I've never worn trousers in my life."

Aunt Sarah laughed. "Your visits to town must be newsworthy events," she said.

His laugh joined hers. "I assure you I'm never without my britches."

Aunt Sarah turned toward Mary. "Make it britches, then," she said.

It felt good to hear Father laugh. I was grateful to Aunt Sarah for making it happen, but also jealous that I'd been unable to achieve the same feat.

"You are looking well," Aunt Sarah told him. "Far better than I expected after Ash's report."

I agreed. The ague had lifted, and Father was stronger, steadier on his feet than he had been in days.

"I owe it to you and your fine meal," he told her. "I suspect Stony and I shall be returned to Victoria in record time." Stony was Father's horse; he had followed us to town, tied to the back of the carriage.

"Victoria is being cared for by our neighbor to the north," I explained to Aunt Sarah, "but Father insists that Victoria is temperamental and responds only to familiar hands at milking time. Too rough a touch and she won't give a drop, he says."

"It puts her in a bad mood," he said, drawing out the double *o* in *mood,* making it sound like a moo.

I knew what was happening. It was what always happened when Father felt he was fenced in with no way out. He'd get such an itch to move, to be free, he'd practically paw at the ground. If our winters weren't so vicious, and the requirements of fatherhood so confining, I think he could have lived in the woods without regret or unfilled need. Sometimes it hurt me to know that when he felt his best, he was least willing to stay at my side.

"Well," she told him, "you must at least stay until Monday—Rebecca's first day at school."

* * *

23

Mary, Aunt Sarah's servant girl, looked to be my age or, at the very most, seventeen. She moved silently through the house, averting her eyes whenever she encountered one of us. And when she spoke, it was in partial sentences that reminded me of the conversations I had had with the Indians who lived by the river.

"Dress," she said simply when she brought a newly sewn frock to my room. She had worked steadily at it all of Sunday so that it would be finished in time for my introduction at school.

"Oh, Mary, thank you! It is beautiful." And that it was, for she had deviated considerably from the plain design of my existing wardrobe, adding fashionable flourishes—under, I rightly assumed, my aunt's direction. The sleeves, poufed at the shoulder, tapered to a snug fit at the wrist. The collar stood high and proud, while the skirt fell in soft folds to my ankles. I held my new dress to my frame, admiring the creamy soft color in the mirror.

Mary backed out of the room, her cheeks pink with pleasure or self-consciousness, or a mix of both.

I tried on the dress at once, twisting and turning before the mirror, not quite believing that anything so lovely could truly be mine. I went across the hall to Father's door and tapped lightly.

"Come in," he said, and I did.

He let go that deep laugh of his. "Just look at us, would you? At home, we don't even *have* doors on our bedrooms, and now here we are *knocking* on them—like the finest of folks." But then he stopped laughing and looked at me. "My, aren't you the pretty one?" he said.

I twirled, giving him the view from all angles.

"You will make an entire school fall in love with you," he whispered, leaning close to kiss my forehead.

For a moment, seeing myself by lamplight in the mirror, I thought he might be right.

I rose before dawn on Monday, too excited and nervous to sleep. Beginnings have always frightened me.

While I dressed, Aunt Sarah slipped into my room with a pair of her shoes. The soles were still shiny, the buttons tight, yet she claimed they were old and, if I had no use for them, they would be discarded. I thanked her for the lie by kissing her cheek.

"Let me brush your hair," she begged.

I sat down at the dressing table before the oval mirror and watched as Aunt Sarah swept my hair high in a style so sophisticated, I would never have thought myself advanced enough to wear it. But I liked it. It made me feel like someone else—someone I would like to be.

Aunt Sarah reached into the pocket of her dressing gown and withdrew a cameo brooch, which she pinned just below the center of my collar.

"It's so beautiful," I told her.

"It was your grandmother's. But it looks as if it were made for you."

With the rest of the family still slumbering, Aunt Sarah and I tiptoed down the stairway, to the dining room, giggling like children.

"Shhh . . ." she said, holding a silencing finger to her lips—which, of course, caused us to giggle all the louder.

We heard Mary in the kitchen, busy with breakfast. Soon she added a basket of biscuits to the sugar, but-

25

ter, jam, and large pot of coffee already on the table. She went back to the kitchen then returned immediately with two bowls of oatmeal and a pitcher of cream.

I thanked her for the meal, though I knew that I wouldn't be able to swallow a bite. Aunt Sarah, however, attacked the food with the gusto she exhibited in all her undertakings. She was lathering her second biscuit with strawberry jam when she noticed that I'd managed to down only a partial cup of coffee.

"You don't want your stomach gurgling during geometry, do you?" she asked.

Geometry. That hadn't been taught at the school I had attended in the woods. Some nights Father sat with me after dinner, trying to show me what his father had taught him about the relationship of lines and angles. But it always seemed a muddle to me.

"What other subjects will I study?"

"Wonderful things . . . algebra, bookkeeping, elocution, rhetoric, history," she said, counting the topics off on her fingers. There were so many, she had to use her other hand: "Government, mental philosophy, moral philosophy, Latin, Greek, and . . . oh dear, I need my toes!"

"Will there be literature?"

"I would think so."

"And composition?"

"Certainly."

"Good."

"I remember now," Aunt Sarah said. "I remember how proud Hannah was of your spelling."

"I've won the competition every year," I said, hoping it sounded more like a statement of fact than a boast. "Mrs. Hatcher taught me to read the dictionary like a novel, paying particular attention to the words I didn't know. She told me to learn them—learn how they're spelled, learn what they mean, learn to use them in conversation."

"Goodness. That seems like an awful lot of work," she said, and I knew she meant it. My aunt was not one to puzzle things out or to follow a plan. She always acted on impulse, generally with excellent results.

"For me, it is play. I love the look of words on a page and the individual letters, too. I asked Mother to teach me to make a sampler. I wanted to do the alphabet in colorful threads and intricate stitches." I paused, thinking perhaps my aunt would volunteer herself as teacher.

"Heavens, no. I know what you're thinking, but no, I could never show you how. Needlework is too solitary, too demanding of time. I've never learned it."

I was struck by how different my mother and her sister were. My mother stole hours from her already bursting days so that she might work privately at her embroidery, but my aunt could not have imagined an evening without inviting in guests or going calling on neighbors. My mother loved the wildflowers and bees, the snakelike curves of the river and the soothing palette of mid-autumn. My aunt preferred the softness of velvet, the heft of gold, the thoughts expressed by others rather than her own. Yet I loved them both, perhaps even equally, but differently. I felt that my mother had protected me, but that I was supposed to protect my aunt. So it surprised me when she mentioned that she would accompany me to

27

school, to introduce me to Matthew Halcomb, the director.

"Your uncle went to see him, to sign the enrollment papers and pay the tuition," she said. "But I want to take you there the first day."

"Will Mr. Halcomb be my instructor?"

"No. Your instructor is a young man from the East. This is his first semester here. We don't know him."

By "we," I knew that Aunt Sarah was referring to more than just herself and Uncle Ash. She was including her entire circle of friends—the ones whose opinions, in her mind, were the only ones that mattered.

Although the calendar said September, the morning air felt more like November. Aunt Sarah lent me her black woolen wrap. As we approached the school, I thought that we must look like a pair of Sarahs. Not only was I wearing her wrap, I had on a pair of shoes she had donated from her collection. I hoped that we wouldn't encounter anyone who was well acquainted with her accessories.

We passed no other students on the way to the school or in the building. After some searching, we found Mr. Halcomb's office, but the door was closed and locked.

"I wonder how early we are," I said.

"Early enough to look around."

The building stood three stories high, with a bell tower rising from the roof. On the lower floor, several large classrooms opened onto a central hall. We peeked through the glass in each of the doors, but the rooms were empty.

"Let's try upstairs," Aunt Sarah suggested.

We climbed all the way to the third floor. "It seems calisthenics is part of the curriculum, too," Aunt Sarah laughed.

At the top of the stairs we saw an open door and heard movement inside the room. I held back, but Aunt Sarah bustled in as if she belonged there.

"Excuse me, sir," she said. "We are looking for Mr. Halcomb."

A tall rail of a man—no more than twenty or twenty-one years old—looked up from the book that lay open on his desk. There was a slowness about him, a deliberate delay in response, that gave him the air of one just awakening from a deep slumber.

"Mr. Halcomb?" he repeated, scooting his chair back and coming slowly to his feet.

I understood his fog. I've returned just as reluctantly from a page when interrupted while reading.

"Mr. Halcomb's office is on the first floor," the young man said. "But he is seldom here so early. I've just come in to start the stove. Perhaps I can help you," he suggested.

By then I was fully in the room. The young man acknowledged me with a slight nod.

"This is my niece," Aunt Sarah explained. "She's to begin school here today."

The young man smiled and offered his hand. "Then you must be Rebecca," he said. "I'm William, your instructor."

"Mr. Williams?" I asked.

"No, just William. William Root. I ask my students to call me by my first name."

The rise in Aunt Sarah's brow was almost imperceptible, but it was a gesture I recognized at once

29

because my mother used to express reservation in the same way. How many times had I seen that silent symbol of rebuff or hesitation!

"School has changed since I attended," she said.

"Informality is the exception, not the rule here," he said.

I liked him, though I didn't know if I could adapt to addressing my instructor with such familiarity.

"You may hang your wrap on a peg," he told me, indicating a row of wooden pegs on one wall. "Then I will show you your books."

Mr. Root—William—paid little attention to Aunt Sarah. At any rate, less notice than she was accustomed to receiving, so I knew it was with a tinge of hurt that she said, "It appears I'm not needed here."

William looked at her, his face soft and kind, the way I've always imagined a saint's must be. "Thank you for enrolling Rebecca in our school."

He took the hand Aunt Sarah extended. "I look forward to her contributions this term," he said.

"She's a remarkable speller, Mr. Root. You may wish to enter her in the school's competition."

My face felt flushed and hot.

William turned his attention toward me. "Have you entered competitions before?"

"Yes, of course she has," Aunt Sarah said. "Rebecca, spell something for him."

I could remember no other time when I had felt so thoroughly embarrassed.

"Spell *incompetent*," she said.

I wished that I could disappear. I knew William had failed Aunt Sarah's congeniality test—but, thankfully, he seemed unaware that she was making fun at his expense. His face retained its almost holy glow of good humor.

I heard motion behind me and turned to see two girls and a boy—all approximately my age—entering the room. I smiled and they smiled back. They put their coats on pegs, then sat down at desks as if they knew where they belonged. William said he would wait for the entire class to arrive before introducing me. First, he said, he would show me the textbooks.

Again, Aunt Sarah mentioned that she could see how little she was needed. She brushed my cheek with a kiss and said her good-byes.

When we could no longer hear the tap of her shoes in the corridor or on the stair, William looked at me for what seemed like several seconds. I was not made uncomfortable by his attention. I was certain that I knew his heart—his kindliness and his sensibility. He meant me no offense. He was simply as struck as I by the speed of our rapport.

"I think we shall be good friends, Rebecca," William said at last.

I agreed, but in silence, knowing it was unnecessary to say that I felt we were friends already. He had known it even before I had, at the very first moment. Only minutes had passed since I had entered his classroom . . . only minutes since I had watched that slow lift of his head at the sound of Aunt Sarah's voice. But already I knew, without being told and without having to learn through experience, that I could trust William Root as fully as I trusted my father.

That was important, because I considered trust the highest compliment I could pay another. But it was also important for another reason. I knew, without knowing how I knew, that I would call upon that trust in a moment of desperate need. And I suspected that moment would not be far away.

Four

We sat down to a supper of chicken, squash, dark bread, and custard.

"My new school is perfect," I told the others. "We had such a wonderful time today, the minutes whirled by faster than a tornado. When the closing bell rang, I felt as if I had been there no more than an hour."

Aunt Sarah said, "I hope you made new friends."

"Oh yes. *Many.* Margaret Bird, Lucinda Spears, Anna Thorndike, Catherine Eslin, Kathleen Leary . . ."

"Whoa!" Father laughed. "Are there no males in that school of yours?"

"Richard Collins is nice," I told him. "And Henry Evans, Jonathan Moffett, and . . ."

Everyone's smile grew broader as my list of names grew longer. "You mark my word," Aunt Sarah said, "boys will be first on her list soon enough."

Father laughed again. It felt good to see his mood markedly improved. Shortly before Aunt Sarah called us to supper, I discovered him walking in the meadow behind the house. He looked as lonesome as he had at home. I wondered how much of the smile he wore at the table was sincere—and how much was for his host's and hostess's benefit.

"I believe I learned more today than I did in all my years with Mrs. Hatcher."

"Mrs. Hatcher was a fine teacher," Father said.

"I agree. I do not mean to belittle her or to disparage my other school in any way. I mean only to express how exceptional the new school is."

"It does have an admirable reputation," Uncle Ash said to Father.

"Ash serves as treasurer," Aunt Sarah added. Then she turned to me and asked if I had decided on a best friend yet.

"Margaret Bird," I told her without hesitation. "She's beautiful and brilliant, and has invited me to come to her house after school tomorrow. She plays the piano and wants me to hear."

"It sounds as if Mary had better sew more dresses," Aunt Sarah said. "You can't be wearing the same one very time you're invited somewhere."

Earlier, when I returned from school, I had found two new dresses lying on my bed. "Mary has done quite enough already," I insisted. "I now own three new dresses. That's enough to last me until . . ."

"Thursday," Aunt Sarah broke in.

Uncle Ash asked what was the most interesting thing I had learned at school that day.

"William told us that George Washington was a bit of a snob."

"I don't know that we should speak of our first president in such a way."

"But he *was* a snob. William said he made it a rule that when people came before him, they had to remain standing the entire time—as if they were in the presence of royalty."

"Who is this William you mention?" Father asked.

"William Root, my instructor."

"Oh?"

Aunt Sarah, Uncle Ash, and Father exchanged indecipherable glances.

"Yes," Aunt Sarah said. "I had the, uh, pleasure of meeting Mr. Root this morning. I don't think he knows that you are the school's treasurer, Ash—or that you control his salary."

It appeared that Aunt Sarah was more wounded than I had first realized by William's interest—or lack thereof—in her. As a bona fide beauty, a banker's wife, and a hostess widely recognized for the quality of her entertaining, she must have found his detachment deflating.

"Imagine my surprise," she went on, "when he said that he prefers his students to call him by his first name."

"Perhaps we ought to invite Mr. Root to supper," Uncle Ash suggested. "I would enjoy taking a look at the fellow."

"So would I, but that is a meal I must miss," Father announced. "I plan to leave tomorrow."

"Why tomorrow?" I asked, hoping my question didn't sound like the complaint it was.

Father looked first at Uncle Ash, then Aunt Sarah. He put his hand over hers and said, "Your hospitality is the most congenial I have ever known. But I was not born to such fine surroundings. I belong in the forest."

I knew that symptom well. How often had he told Mother the same thing, saying "cabin" instead of "surroundings"? That yearning of his for the forest was cyclical, peaking in the autumn and the spring— the two best times of the year to hunt bears. Earlier, when walking from school back to Aunt Sarah's, I'd noticed the heaviness of the clouds off in the direction of the river. Rain looked to be only a few hours away. The easiest time to track a bear is when the ground is soft enough—and wet enough—to indent under the weight of his paws.

"I'm told bear pelts are up to six or seven dollars now," Father said.

"But you don't need money," Aunt Sarah said. "You have everything you need right here."

"I don't have the forest."

Aunt Sarah pulled her hand away from his.

"Don't be angry with me," he pleaded. "I'll bring bear meat with me when I haul the pelts to town."

I felt at least a little regret that I wasn't going with him. When I was still a tiny child, barely able to form sentences, Father began teaching me the secrets of tracking. "If it's a bear you want," he explained, "watch for his droppings. If they're moist, he's nearby. Look for fresh claw marks in the tree trunks, too—and hairs caught on low-lying branches."

"Just remember that bears can outrun men," I said, but I was instantly sorry. Those words had come into my mind without thought or plan because they were the ones Mother had always called out to him as he left with his gun.

Father's face looked stricken for a moment, but only a moment. "Maybe so," he said. "But they can't out*shoot* me."

I felt grateful when the others laughed. It meant that Aunt Sarah had forgiven Father. And Father had forgiven me.

Father was dressed, fed, and on his way before I awakened the next morning. I hurried from my room to his, but found the door open, the bed made, and his belongings removed. Standing at the top of the stairs, I listened to the noises below. Only Aunt Sarah's voice, and Uncle Ash's, floated up to me.

I guessed that Father was headed toward Fulton County. Bears were rare in our area, but abundant there. Fulton County was also richer in deer, but Father preferred not to hunt for them where the challenge was so empty. Deer were so plentiful, farmers had to chase them from their barnyards lest they devour all the food that had been put out for the farm animals. A year earlier, Father had returned with exciting tales of how heavily populated those distant woods were—telling Mother and me about packs of 300 wolves that roamed together. He said he'd even seen enough wild turkeys to cover an entire acre. But the wild hogs were his greatest fear. To avoid an attack, there was nothing he could do but run to a tree and scale it quickly. But he had to be certain his tree was solid. Hogs can easily uproot a frail one. From his perch on high, Father would drop a piece of his clothing to the ground so that the hogs could sniff it and tear it to pieces. Because that satisfied them as much as a piece of his flesh would have, they would then move on in search of other prey.

As I imagined Father making his way south, I remembered the many times when I had tramped along beside him, entrusted with the essential task of watching for snakes. A fellow we knew stepped in a nest of blue racers once. When he lifted his foot, he found five of the critters coiled round it. I wondered who would be Father's lookout now that I was a city girl.

While trying to fall asleep the night before, I had lectured myself on the need to awaken early, before Father could escape without a hug. It was vital for me to see him—not just because I loved him, but because it was my fifteenth birthday. I'd never had a birthday before when I didn't see him.

I thought back to the celebration we'd enjoyed one year earlier—when I still had a mother, and my home was still in the woods. The three of us—Mother, Father, and I—had taken a lunch to the riverbank, where we sat in the shade of a sycamore tree, immersed in the glorious Indian summer weather. Nearby, fishermen speared muskellunge and black bass by the dozens. Remembering it with such clarity, there was nothing I wouldn't have given to go back to that day, that time.

The bleakness of my mood must have been obvious when I joined Aunt Sarah and Uncle Ash in the dining room for breakfast. But it improved considerably when I pulled out my chair from the table and saw a wrapped package on the seat.

"Happy birthday," Aunt Sarah said.

"My, my. Fifteen years old already," Uncle Ash said, shaking his head and smiling.

"I didn't know that you knew," I said.

"We *didn't,*" Aunt Sarah explained, "until your Father told us. He's the one who put that gift on your chair."

"Father?" I was surprised. He had said nothing to me about it. "I thought he forgot."

"Not at all," Uncle Ash said. "He worked on your gift most of the day Sunday, and a great deal of yesterday."

I peeled the paper away and found a beautiful, handcrafted harmonica. On a small note that was enclosed Father had written: *Rebecca, I will teach you to play this when I come to town next time. Happy birthday. With love, Your father.*

"What a gift to give a young lady," Aunt Sarah said. She was smiling, but I could tell that she was genuinely bewildered.

"I've been begging for this forever. He never had the time to do a proper job of making one, he said. But look . . . look how perfect it is!" Seeing the clean lines and smooth surfaces of the harmonica was such a joy, it nearly made up for the sadness I felt at not seeing Father before he left. Nearly.

"You are an unusual girl," Uncle Ash said.

"After school we can go to the shops on Main Street," Aunt Sarah suggested. "You can pick out any gift you like."

I started to thank her, but then remembered that I had an invitation to go to Margaret Bird's house after school.

"Could we do that tomorrow instead?" I asked. "I told Margaret I would come to her house this afternoon to listen to her play the piano."

"Yes, of course. I forgot. You must take your harmonica and make an orchestra."

I had already decided to tuck the harmonica into my pocket. I wanted to show it to everyone—Margaret, William, everyone at school. In my mind, I could hear music playing . . . lively music that I hoped someday I would learn to play on my harmonica. But the music in my mind gradually changed tone until it became ethereal, haunting, more reflective of my earlier mood. I wondered if that could have been how Shut-nok's song sounded so many years ago, as it echoed in the grove.

I shall always remember my fifteenth birthday as a day that was brimming over with new information. My mind was filled with vivid pictures of the past, beginning where William's history lecture did—in the Ice Age.

He described how our land, our very neighborhood, had once been covered with massive sheets of ice. It was thousands of years ago, he said. He told us how men had followed the receding ice, moving onto the thawed patches of land that emerged. These were the Mound Builders, he said—people surprisingly like us. They grew crops, wove cloth, made bricks, and tempered copper. William also told us that animals shaped much like today's elephants once lived right here. Mastodons, he called them.

William told us we learned these things from archaeologists who had dug down into the ground as much as sixteen feet or even more, unearthing skeletons, tools, and jewelry.

I had grown up believing that the Indians were the first men here, but there was William—telling us that others had been here *centuries* earlier. I wondered how many of the other things that I'd been accepting as fact were, after all, untrue.

William's purpose in telling us about the Mound Builders was to warn us about extinction. "The Mound Builders and the mastodons no longer walk the earth," he said. "We have only buried mementos to remind us that they were ever here. And if we aren't careful, that could happen to the Indians, too. Or to us."

He went on to describe the overwhelming loss of life that accompanies war. "It's a wonder that any Indians survived the War of 1812. And it's possible that we white men will be less victorious in the next battle we initiate. The example of the Mound Builders shows us that an entire tribe of people can disappear just like that," he said, snapping his fingers.

40

Then William held up a picture—a delicate hand-painted portrait of an egret. As it happens, that's my favorite bird. I love its long, gracefully curved neck . . . its bright yellow beak . . . and the beauty of its white-feathered body atop long, spindlelike legs. How I love to see an egret spread its magnificent wings. They reach out more than two feet on each side. I have seen huge flocks of them line the beaches of Maumee Bay, especially in July and August. But William warned us that even this delightful creature could cease to be.

"Women insist on having egret plumes in their hats," he explained, "giving no thought to what that means to the egret population. We are killing them for commercial purposes far faster than they can reproduce."

I noticed that Margaret Bird had tears in her eyes, but most of the boys in the classroom looked as if they would have rather been talking about war again.

Father had always been less enthusiastic about fighting and killing than most other males appeared to be. For example, he would go miles out of his way to avoid passing the Kramer farm after he and Mr. Kramer had their differences over the treatment of Indians. Mr. Kramer wanted to expand his land to include a settlement where twelve or fifteen of them lived. He spoke with Father about forcing them out by whatever means necessary so that the two of them could share the land. But Father told Mr. Kramer to leave our property and never speak to him again of such a barbaric plan.

I agreed with Father. The Indians had never meant us harm. They wanted only to fish, make maple sugar, and raise their corn and beans. In peace. When the weather turned bitter cold, we could expect whole

41

families of them to appear at our cabin door, asking to come in and spend the night. And Father could always be counted on to say yes. They slept on the floor, in front of the fire, never giving us any trouble (except once—when a brave had to be stopped from bringing his shivering pony into the house).

I remember one night when the wind was colder than ice. The Indian family staying in our cabin included a man, a woman, and their infant son. I watched as the woman sat down on the heated hearth and placed her child beside her. She raked out some of the ashes from the fire, taking care to separate them from the hot coals. Then she scooped up the warm ashes with her hands and covered her baby with them. I could hear his coo of contentment.

There was only one Indian who tried Father's patience. He came to our cabin day after day begging for some of our cider. It was exceptionally good that year. In the beginning, Father was happy to oblige. But the begging became so frequent, Father finally told the man he could have no more—unless he carried it away in a basket. I remember how Father laughed at the impossibility of the challenge he'd given the man. The Indian left our land, and we thought that was the last we would see of him. But a few days later, he returned with a basket that was coated with ice. He told us that he had dipped it in water which he let freeze, then he repeated the process over and over until there were enough layers of ice to make the vessel solid. Father had no choice but to fill it, and he did so happily.

The thought that Indians might someday be extinct like the Mound Builders—and that egrets might cease to be simply because women must have plumes—had put me in such a somber mood, Margaret asked if I would rather come to her house on another day. But I assured her that I looked forward to the visit. We left school together, walking slowly toward her house, discussing all we had just learned about birds, battles, and bones.

As we approached the steps to Margaret's front porch, a stout woman appeared in the doorway. "I was worried," she said. "You're late today."

"I'm sorry," Margaret said. "We stayed after, talking to William."

"Again?" the woman asked, sounding pained.

"He had pictures in a book we wanted to see ... pictures of egrets."

The woman looked relieved. "Ornithology? That's good. At least he's teaching something worthwhile."

"But his lecture wasn't about birds. Not entirely. He also spoke of ..." I stopped in midsentence because Margaret had nudged me hard with her elbow.

"Spoke of *what?*" the woman asked sounding suddenly alarmed. "Negroes? Slaves? Did he mention the slaves?"

"No, Mother," Margaret said. "He didn't mention them at all. I swear he didn't."

I was surprised to learn that the woman was Margaret's mother. Aunt Sarah had described her as a bright, cheerful woman—but I had seen none of that.

She shook her finger at us, saying, "That man is nothing more than an abolitionist, and don't you forget it."

"Yes, ma'am," Margaret replied.

After Mrs. Bird disappeared back into the house, Margaret asked me if I would mind if she didn't play the piano that day. "I'd rather stay out here," she said, sitting down on the top step of her porch. "I always stay out of Mother's way when she's in such a sour mood."

As I sat down beside her, I said, "Today is my birthday."

"Really? Why didn't you tell me before so I could have planned a party?"

"This *is* a party."

I'd never gone home from school with anyone before, not even back at my old school in the forest. There was always too much work to do after classes.

"I mean a real party with people and presents and cake."

"I already have a wonderful present—a harmonica, from my father."

I could tell by the look on Margaret's face that she didn't see what was so wonderful about that.

"He made it himself," I added.

"Can you play it?"

"Not yet, but someday I will." I was determined not to let Father put off the music lessons, the way Mother had postponed the sewing lessons until it was too late.

"I brought it to school today to show you," I told her. "But then I was so excited about coming to your house, I forgot to get it off the hat shelf when we left."

"You left it at school? Aren't you afraid that someone will take it?"

"Who would take it?" I asked, truly wondering. I wasn't used to the ways of the city yet.

"One of the boys," Margaret said. "Or William."

"William?"

Margaret nodded knowingly. "You can never tell what an abolitionist might do."

At the meetinghouse in the forest, where we went for Sunday services, the circuit preachers who visited the pulpit had sometimes mentioned abolitionists in their sermons. But they had never spoken ill of them. Instead, they told stories about how some of the abolitionists helped slaves make their way to freedom.

"Abolitionists just want to abolish slavery, that's all," I told her.

"That's *all?*" Margaret asked, her eyes wide with surprise. "Don't you know that slaves belong to people? Helping them run away is the same as stealing from the owners."

"But slavery is wrong."

"Whether slavery is right or wrong is beside the point," she said. "It's the stealing that's wrong."

I'd never heard abolitionists described as thieves before. To tell the truth, I'd never given them much thought one way or the other.

"If William would steal another man's slaves, there's no reason why he wouldn't steal your harmonica," Margaret continued.

"How do you know that William is an abolitionist?"

"My father told me," Margaret said. "He's the sheriff. It's his job to capture the runaways and return them to their owners. It's also his job to arrest the abolitionists."

"Then why hasn't he arrested William?"

"You can't arrest a man just for what people say he does. You have to catch him doing it first."

My mind was a jumble of confusion. I had been

brought up just as Margaret had—by parents who had taught me that stealing was wrong. But even so, I couldn't help hoping that William would never be caught.

Five

I arrived early for school the next day. When I entered the room, I saw that William and I were the only ones there.

"You must rise with the rooster," he said.

"And so must you."

He smiled. "You are in time to help me with the stove."

He handed me some sticks of kindling and, together, we urged the embers to light them.

"This was my job at home," I told him. "First thing in the morning, I would start the stove where we did our cooking."

"Where is home? I thought you lived here."

"Well, I do and I don't. My father and I live in the woods. My stay at Aunt Sarah's house is temporary, until the school term is over."

There was a wistful look on William's face. "I think I would like living in the woods," he said. "I'm from the East, where there's such a thing as a hill or two. I never knew until I reached Ohio just how flat the land could be."

"You should see where we live. There are plenty of hills."

He gave me a teasing, sideways glance.

"Really," I insisted.

"Perhaps you will show me someday," he said.

"Where do you live?"

"Do you know where the apothecary shop is?"

"Isn't it across the street from my uncle's bank?"

"Yes, that's the one. I have the small apartment that's above the shop."

The fire was burning well by then. "The heat feels good, doesn't it?" I said.

Again, the morning air was damp and cold, giving us a touch of winter several weeks ahead of schedule—such a change from the mosquitoes and heat that had defined my life only a week earlier.

"Wait until November and December," he said. "This room will be so cold by then, shivering is the only thing that will keep us awake."

"Shivering or not," I told William, "I could never sleep through one of your lectures."

He gave me a quick look, appraising my sincerity. "Thank you, Rebecca. That means a great deal to me."

When the flames finally began to leap, I turned toward the shelf that sat just above the pegs where our coats were hung—the hat shelf. I wanted to get my harmonica so that I could show it to William. But I could see that the shelf was empty, except for William's hat. I continued to stare at the shelf, remembering Margaret's warning about our teacher. Behind me, I could hear William settling down in the chair at his desk.

"Are you looking for this?" he asked.

When I turned around, I saw that he had my harmonica. A wave of relief washed over me. "I thought it was gone."

"I found it when I came in this morning. It's very beautiful."

I nodded, agreeing. "My father made it for me. My birthday was yesterday."

"You must be about fifteen," William said. He told me that he remembered his fifteenth year as a happy time.

"You make it sound as if it were centuries ago," I said.

"Sometimes it feels that way." He sighed. There was a faraway look in his eyes.

After a long pause, he added, "When we're young, we want to change the world, but before we realize it, just the opposite has happened—the world has changed us."

There was a long silence that I didn't know how to fill.

William had laid the harmonica down on his desk. I picked it up and was about to push it into the pocket of my cape when he asked if I would play it for him.

"I don't know how," I admitted. "Father says he'll teach me."

"May I try?" William asked.

I placed the harmonica in his extended hand. He took it to his lips and began to play a lovely melody unlike any I had ever heard before. It was light, with notes that spoke as clearly as words—describing the best things I had known in my life. Sunsets, waterfalls, fresh-baked muffins.

"That was beautiful," I said when he stopped. "What was it?"

"I don't know."

"But you just played it."

"I made it up."

"It was so soft and sweet. I really loved it."

"Did you?" he asked. "Then we will call it 'Rebecca's Song.' "

"Thank you," I said. "You are very nice. I don't understand why everyone can't see that."

Oh dear. I hadn't meant to say that. The words were out before I could stop them. "I'm sorry," I said.

"Has someone said that I'm not nice?" he asked, looking bemused.

A blush took control of my face as he waited for my response.

"Someone said that you're . . ." My voice faltered.

"That I'm what, Rebecca?"

"An abolitionist," I said, almost whispering.

When I saw his reaction, I wished that I could somehow reclaim my words. His jaw was set in a firm line and his eyes seemed to lose their light. I was certain that I had made a terrible mistake. From the first day that I saw William, I had known that I could trust him with anything, any secret, but still I felt afraid of his anger—especially since my words had caused it.

"Who said that about me?" he asked.

The only sounds in the room were the crackle and pop of the fire and the beat of my heart. "Mrs. Bird," I said. "Margaret's mother."

"I see," he said, nodding his head. "What else did she say?"

"Only that."

"What did it mean to you when she called me an abolitionist? Did you think less of me? Or more?"

"I didn't know what to think. It isn't right to steal another person's property."

"Come here, Rebecca," he said.

I hesitated.

"Please."

I went nearly to the desk, careful to remain a few feet away.

"No," he said. "Come here, beside me. I want to show you something."

I did as he directed, and watched as he opened his bottom desk drawer. There, alone, lay a small but thick book with a well-worn blue cover.

William looked straight at me with unwavering eyes and no hint of a smile. "This book is always kept right here. I cannot give it to you to read because I have promised the director of the school I will not force—or even encourage—students to adopt certain beliefs which I brought with me when I accepted this teaching position."

I nodded as if I understood, but I didn't.

"I cannot give you this book," he repeated, "but neither will I stop you from taking it. You know where it is."

As I stared at the book, he placed his hand on it as gently as a mother might stroke her favorite child's hair. "If you truly want to know what is right and what is wrong," he said, "I promise you that you will find the answer here."

"Mary is sick," Aunt Sarah announced when I came in from school. "You and I must cook supper."

I didn't remind her that she had promised to take me shopping that afternoon for a belated birthday gift.

51

"I've prepared a basket of tea cakes and side pork, raisin bread and sweet butter," she said. "Will you be a dear and take it to poor Mary?"

Mary lived alone in a modest, but solid, one-room building that stood between the main house and the barn. I tried to peek in the window, to see if she was awake, but the curtains were pulled closed. I'd never seen them that way before.

I knocked several times before Mary opened her door. She did not invite me in. Rather, she seemed to be blocking my entrance.

"I've brought you some food," I said, offering the basket.

"Thank you." Her voice was barely audible. She grasped the basket, then pushed the door with surprising speed—closing it fully even before I had finished turning back toward the house.

"How is she?" Aunt Sarah asked.

"She didn't say."

I decided not to tell Aunt Sarah that I thought her poor, sick Mary looked remarkably well.

After school was let out on Thursday, I stayed behind, watching all the other students leave. When there was no one left in the room except William and me, he looked at me expectantly—as if waiting for me to speak. I said nothing, but kept glancing toward his desk.

William was standing by the window. After a few moments he moved to the back of the room. I waited until he had continued on out into the hallway. Then I hurried to his desk and opened the bottom drawer. I reached in and took out the thick blue book that he had shown me the day before. Turning its spine upward, I read the title: *Uncle Tom's Cabin*. The author's name was Harriet Beecher Stowe.

I hid the book inside my cloak, hugging it tight against my body as I hurried from the room.

Six

When I came in from school, I slipped upstairs before saying hello to Aunt Sarah—and before removing the cloak that covered William's book. I went directly to my room, closed the door, and withdrew *Uncle Tom's Cabin* from its hiding place. I put it under my pillow (by patting down the feather stuffing a bit, I was able to disguise the suspicious bump it made).

As noiselessly as a butterfly, I moved slowly down the stairs, but Aunt Sarah, who was passing through the central hallway from one room to another, spied me.

"Rebecca! You startled me. What are you doing?"

I tried the obvious: "Coming downstairs."

"But why are you wearing your cloak?"

"It's your cloak, Aunt Sarah," I said, stalling.

"Why haven't you taken it off? Why didn't you tell me you were home from school?"

Lies generally don't come tumbling into my mind before the truth, so it took me a moment to answer. "I . . . I was looking for . . . for my, uh . . . my harmonica," I said. Then, gathering steam, I added, "I forgot to show it to Margaret when I was at her house the other day. I was hoping I could take it there now."

Aunt Sarah smiled—but, because it was a believing, trusting smile, I felt terrible.

"I thought we would go shopping today—for your birthday gift," she said. She sounded disappointed.

"Oh yes," I said, trying to appear excited. "I would love to do that." But the fact was, I would have preferred by far to remain at home and read my book.

Because the primary shopping district was so close to Aunt Sarah's house, we decided to walk rather than put Horace to the trouble of outfitting the carriage. The slight mist in the air would have felt good had it not been for the accompanying chill.

"Don't you have Indian summer in the city?" I asked.

Aunt Sarah sighed. "That is one of the things I miss most about growing up in the woods—how near to God's Heaven it is. But yes, of course, we have Indian summer. It's just not as beautiful. There are too many houses and buildings spoiling the view."

I was surprised by her words. I had always assumed that nothing was beautiful in Aunt Sarah's eyes unless it was expensive and man-made.

"Do you remember how the rabbits run through the fields and the deer try to peek in your cabin windows?" she asked.

I nodded.

"That's what I remember best about my last trip to see your mother. I tried to bring her back home with me, for a visit, but she said summer in the woods was something she couldn't bear to miss."

I knew we were both wondering the same thing as we walked on in silence. Would things have turned out differently if Mother had gone home with Aunt

Sarah? Would the cholera have passed her by? Would I be back in the woods with her now, sharing her grief over the many beloved neighbors who were taken?

"The illness stalked us here, too," Aunt Sarah said, as if reading my mind. "House to house it went, sometimes killing whole families. Ash didn't go to the bank for days. He just closed it down, and we stayed locked up in the house until the danger passed—Ash, Mary, Horace, and me."

"Where does Horace live?"

"I don't know. Over there somewhere," she said, dismissing the question, waving her hand toward the lesser side of town.

"Does he have a family?"

"Goodness yes! A wife and eight children."

I didn't ask the question I wanted to ask—but, as it happened, I didn't need to.

"He *wanted* to go home, to be with his wife and children," Aunt Sarah said. "But I . . . well, Ash and I . . . we couldn't let him go."

"Oh?" I was wondering why Horace didn't defy them and leave on his own.

"Ash told Horace he would have no employment to return to if he left us at such a time. We needed someone to carry the wood indoors . . . someone to take care of the horses and chickens."

I looked at her without saying anything.

Again, it seemed she could read my thoughts. "Well, I couldn't let *Ashley* go outdoors. There was no telling where the cholera might be."

We went to only one shop that day—Mrs. Sanford's House of Millinery and Fashions. Mrs. Sanford looked more like a customer than a clerk. She

56

seemed to glide, not walk, wearing a dress of iridescent fabric. It changed from blue to purple to blue-green as she moved. I knew how rude I was being, but I couldn't help myself: I stared openly.

"Show her the dress we discussed, Susan," Aunt Sarah directed.

Mrs. Sanford stepped into a back room then returned with a dress the color of chocolate. Around the rim of the neckline and at the tips of the sleeves there was sewn an intricate lace that was more beautiful than any other I had ever seen. Pinned to it was a brooch of white beads.

"Genuine pearls," Mrs. Sanford assured us.

Aunt Sarah took the dress from Mrs. Sanford and held it to me. "It was made for you. Try it on," she said.

I went into the fitting room and changed clothes, worrying the entire time about the cost of such an elegant gift. Because it was too formal for school, I doubted that there would ever be an occasion when I could wear it. It would certainly never come out of my trunk once I returned to the woods. But, oh, it *was* lovely. And Aunt Sarah was right—it was made for me. It fit perfectly, flaring outward from the waist down, but looking as if it were molded to my form from the waist up.

"We'll take it," Aunt Sarah announced as soon as she saw me.

"But Aunt Sarah . . ."

"That's final." She turned toward Mrs. Sanford and said, "Wrap it up, Susan."

"But I have no place to wear it," I insisted.

"Hush, Rebecca. I'm planning a party. I want my friends to meet you—so you'll *need* a party dress, don't you see?"

"Perhaps a more festive color would be appropriate," Mrs. Sanford suggested.

"No, no, this one is just right," Aunt Sarah told her. "Look how burnished her skin is—it's all those months of going bareheaded in the sun. If we put her in a light color, the contrast would make her look almost Indian."

No one had ever told me that about myself before. I studied my image in Mrs. Sanford's full-length mirror. Maybe Aunt Sarah was right, I decided.

"Smile," Aunt Sarah said.

I turned toward her and did as she asked.

"No, not at me," she laughed. "At yourself, in the mirror—I want you to see how the white of your teeth glows against the dark of your skin."

Yes, she was definitely right. I wondered if my friends at school had noticed how different I was from them. Perhaps not. After all, I hadn't noticed how pale they were beside me.

I excused myself from the supper table that evening, claiming exhaustion. "I think I'll go upstairs early," I said.

"Well, you have had quite a day," Aunt Sarah agreed. "All those hours at school, then a walk to the store and back . . ."

"Yes," I said, stifling an artificial yawn.

I went to the other side of the table to give Uncle Ash a kiss good night. "Thank you for the birthday dress," I told him. "I love it."

Aunt Sarah wished me sweet dreams as I left the room. In the hallway, I encountered Mary—but she skittered away like a frightened mouse.

Alone in my room, I removed the coverlet from my bed and rolled it lengthwise until it looked like a

58

large window shade in the open position. I used it to cover the gap between the bottom of my door and the floor. That way, Aunt Sarah and Uncle Ash wouldn't see that my lamp was burning when they came upstairs.

I took the book out from under the pillow and crawled into bed, eager to see what the pages contained. When I began reading, the sky was growing dark—and by the time I finished the final page, it was turning light again. But I didn't feel tired. I felt enlivened by what I had read and eager to discuss it with William.

As I had two other mornings that week, I dressed and left the house needlessly early—this time without breakfast (Aunt Sarah and Uncle Ash hadn't come down yet, so there was no one to complain or stop me). Just as it had entered the house, the book left under the cover of my cloak.

I arrived at school, but found it to be empty. The morning air felt less biting than it had earlier in the week. I correctly guessed that William had seen no need for a fire and that he would arrive later than usual. The door to our classroom was unlocked, so I went in, put my cloak on a peg, and placed the book in William's bottom drawer.

I went to the window and looked out at the rooftops of houses—the cupolas and widows' walks, the gingerbread fretwork that set these dwellings so apart from the cabins in the woods. I thought how easily I'd become attached to the large rooms and polished floors of Aunt Sarah's home . . . the ferns, the marble-top chests, the Oriental rugs. How easy it was to come downstairs to a prepared breakfast, a cup of steaming coffee, rather than kindling up the fire myself and searching out eggs in the barn. I thought of the people I'd met in Mrs. Stowe's wonderful book . . . people like Aunt Sarah and Uncle Ash, rich people relying on others to do their work. I wondered how much like them I was on the inside—in my heart, if not my purse.

I'd wept the night before, not even realizing it at first—I was that caught up in the story of Eliza, a Negress, a slave woman whose owner meant to sell her young son away from her just to settle a debt with another slave owner. Eliza escaped from Kentucky, a slave state, to Ohio, a free state. She did it in the dark of a winter night, riding the river on an ice floe. White people helped her, ensuring her safe passage onward to freedom in Canada, ignoring the federal law that threatened them with a lengthy jail term and a heavy fine for doing so. The law agreed with Margaret that helping a man's slaves escape was the same as stealing his property—even if you did so in a state where there was no slavery. That was why Eliza could not be truly free until she had reached Canadian soil.

The South, where slavery was as common as cornfields were here, was like a myth to me, a made-up place where rich people were allowed to own poor people, so long as their skin was dark. But Mrs. Stowe's book persuaded me that the South was real, and not just a fabled place freemen described when they settled in the North. She said she had taken her characters from life. She had known the people herself, or she knew someone else who had known them—the heartless auctioneers who sold children away from their mothers, husbands away from their wives, and the greedy plantation owners who purchased this inexpensive labor for no one's gain but their own.

60

Mrs. Stowe said she also knew the men and women who broke man's law, choosing instead to enforce God's law that we should love one another— brave men and women who opened their homes to slaves on the run, providing them with shelter and transportation as they made their way to freedom. This network of safe houses was called the Underground Railroad—though it seldom involved a train, and, except for a few tunnels, travel was conducted above ground. It was a poetic name meaning "secret transportation."

Mrs. Stowe's book brought the tragedy of slavery to life for me. Her pen touched my heart in a way that it had never been touched before, and I needed to tell William. I needed to thank him for sharing his book.

I also needed to tell him what else I had learned: that abolitionists aren't thieves. They don't take; they give. They wish for, and work toward, the end of slavery. They believe that we should all be free, equally, regardless of our color.

But when William arrived that morning, he was in the company of three other students. They came into the room, laughing and talking, greeting me with warm hellos. Even so, when our eyes met, I knew William understood that I was different, changed from the day before. I knew he understood that I had read Mrs. Stowe's book, and that I had been moved by it.

When we paused in our class schedule at midday, the other students hurried out of the building as they always did, eager to return home for lunch. But I remained in the room with William.

I approached his desk.

"Your book is in the drawer," I said.

He nodded.

"I hope people will call *me* an abolitionist someday," I told him, keeping my voice low for fear of
eavesdroppers.

The smile that overtook William's face was slow,
but beautiful.

Seven

Saturday classes lasted only half the day. Afterward, Margaret and I made good use of the mild weather by taking a lunch of bread and cheese to that place where the town ended and the woods began. We followed a path toward the river until we came to a small clearing where a felled tree provided seating for our picnic.

I noticed that the tree was big around, at its fattest point almost the size of a wagon wheel, but hollow inside.

"Do you know Mr. Metzger?" I asked.

"No."

"The man who used to carry the mail between here and Lima?"

"No."

I giggled. "This log reminds me of him."

Margaret looked rightfully confused.

"The last night that he carried the mail, he stopped in a clearing like this one—to build a fire and bed down. But the wolves kept moving in closer and closer on him, and in such great numbers, he feared for his life. Before the night was over, he crawled into a hollow whitewood log that lay nearby. But the log was too near his fire. It caught the flame, and poor Mr. Metzger was forced out of his hiding place."

Margaret laughed. "What did he do then?"

"I don't know. All I know is he turned in his mailbag and refused to carry another letter."

"Do you think that's true?"

"I saw the mailbag. It was scorched."

"Oooh." Margaret shuddered. "Can you imagine crawling inside a slimy log? All those worms and spiders . . ."

"And splinters." I shuddered, too.

Margaret's mood grew serious. "Tell me about living in the woods."

"You just live, that's all."

"Is it true about the snakes?"

"The blue racers? Yes. Father had to cut one off a fellow once. It was coiled so tight around him, he could barely breathe."

"And is it true about the bears . . . and the wolves . . . and the wild hogs?"

"Yes."

"Then why did you like it there?"

"Because of the snakes and bears and wolves and wild hogs."

"I'm serious. I really don't understand how you could live there," she said.

"I love the woods. Every insect, every bird, every ferocious animal," I told her. But then I corrected myself: "Well, maybe not the *ferocious* ones."

It felt good to laugh with a friend—a genuine friend. In the woods, I lived too far from girls my age to visit with them outside of school. We wrote letters back and forth, but had no money for postage. We delivered them in person when we saw each other in

64

class. Summers would have brimmed with loneliness were it not for all the work that had to be done. I was kept so busy, my heart didn't have time to realize how empty it was at times. But living in Aunt Sarah's house was different. Mary and Horace did all the work.

"What do rich people do with all their time?" I asked.

It was Margaret's turn to giggle. "We're not rich. My father is just the sheriff."

"That sounds exciting."

"But it isn't. Sometimes drunken sailors come ashore down at the docks, but there's little else for him to control," she said. "Except the runaways, of course."

She was talking about the slaves again.

"He has caught more than one of them, you know," she said.

I asked if that was dangerous work.

"Only for the abolitionists. When they get caught they have to pay a big fine."

"How much?"

"As much as a thousand dollars. They can even end up in jail for six months."

"Has your father ever caught an abolitionist?"

"I don't think so. He says they're not easy to catch. A slave is easy because it's a Negro. It looks like a Negro, no matter what. It can't hide what it is. But an abolitionist could be anyone—a white man, a black man, even a woman. Why, we could be passing one on the street every day and never even know it."

"I don't see how anyone could keep something like that secret. People would suspect."

Margaret nodded her head. "I suppose so. Everyone knows that William is an abolitionist."

"Maybe that's just gossip."

"Well, if it is, it's gossip that he started. He talks openly in favor of helping slaves escape—or at least he did until he learned that the school director had no sympathy for his views."

"Mr. Halcomb?" I asked.

"Yes. He knows someone in the East where William used to live—a woman who said she saw William enter a building where an antislavery meeting was going on."

"That's not proof."

"It was good enough for Mr. Halcomb to confront William. Mr. Halcomb told my father all about it. He said William didn't even bother to deny it."

"Well, it's still not proof."

Margaret gave me a long look, then said, "You think a lot of William, don't you?"

"Of course I do. Don't you?"

"Oh yes," Margaret said. "He's wonderful. Before he came here, I hated school. Now I love it."

That interested me. Margaret didn't like abolitionists, but she liked William—even though she thought he was one. And while I didn't like the idea of one person owning another, I liked Margaret—even though she seemed to approve of slavery. The human heart is such a mystery to me.

"It's odd, isn't it," I asked, "liking a person while disapproving of his beliefs?" I was talking as much about Margaret and me as I was about Margaret and William.

"I keep hoping he'll change," she said.

I wanted to tell Margaret that I was wishing the same thing—about her. I wanted to tell her about Mrs. Stowe's story. I wanted her to know how much it had touched me and changed me in the space of just a few hours. But then I remembered how secretive William had been about the book, how careful he had been not to offer it openly. I couldn't betray him. A small voice inside me (one that I have come to trust for the quality of its advice) told me to stand up, to begin talking about the leaves—about how brilliant they were for so early in the year—and to suggest that perhaps we ought to head for home.

Aunt Sarah, Uncle Ash, and I attended church services on Sunday morning, then arrived home by noon to find a welcome surprise. Father was back. He was taking his wagon around back to the barn just as our carriage reached the house.

Father called out my name the moment he saw me.

I ran into his embrace, embarrassed by how happy I felt to see him. When we lived in the woods and he went off to hunt and trap, he never seemed quite so absent as he had when he was no longer at Aunt Sarah's. Or maybe it was Mother's absence that made it more necessary to have him near—I didn't know. All I knew was that I was thrilled to see him.

"You smell like smoke," I told him.

"I made camp with some choppers last night. We sat 'round a hickory fire, telling tales all night long," he said.

"Good. You can share them with us after dinner," Uncle Ash suggested.

"Oh no he can't," I said. "Tonight he's going to teach me to play the harmonica."

Father smiled wide. "Did you like it?"

"I loved it." I got up on my tiptoes to give him a kiss on the cheek. "Thank you."

"You thought I'd never make that harmonica, didn't you?"

"And for good reason," I said with a laugh. "I had to wait fifteen years."

"And now you must wait yet another hour before you can learn learn how to play it," Aunt Sarah said. "Mary will have our Sunday dinner on the table."

We all walked toward the house together. I held tight to Father's arm, not letting go until we reached the doorway. It was as if I thought that by hanging on, I could prevent him from ever leaving me again.

Aunt Sarah had been wrong when she predicted that my harmonica lessons would begin in an hour. Father said he wanted to take his pelts to the man who usually bought them. That surprised me. I had glanced in his wagon when we were outside, but I didn't remember seeing any pelts.

"I promised that I'd deliver them today," he said.

"Not on Sunday," Aunt Sarah protested.

But Father had never been one to put a label on a day. Sunday was like any other day to him. He hadn't been in a church since the day he married Mother. He said he had no time for a religion that pushed people to their knees; he said that his religion was different. It lifted a man up and kept him on his own two feet, no matter what. One day we saw an Indian woman wash a cloth in the river and spread it on a rock to dry. Nearby, a brave stood waist-deep in the water. He was singing a sweet song to the naked baby in his arms. Father put his hand on my shoulder and said, "If you have ever wondered what God is, look at that . . . and if you have ever wondered how He sounds when He speaks to us, listen to that song."

All afternoon I waited for Father to return, and I continued to wait through the evening. How could selling pelts take so long, I wondered. It was already dark when, at last, I heard his heavy boots walking across the front porch.

"Well, look at you," he said.

I was ready for bed—dressed in a flannel gown and robe. I hurried to the dining room to retrieve my harmonica from the buffet then gave it to Father.

He began to play, starting with a mournful tune that I'd never heard before. Aunt Sarah, Uncle Ash, and I leaned back to listen, each of us lost in secret thoughts. Mine were of Mother and her grassy bed in the grove. By the end of the tune, I was so homesick and heartsick, I was certain that I would never recover. But then Father played something cheerful—a song that we all knew, so we sang along. Nearly an hour passed before I realized that I hadn't had a lesson . . . I'd had a concert.

"When am I going to learn?" I asked before going up to bed.

"Soon," he promised.

"When? In another fifteen years?"

He smiled. "No, much sooner. Maybe only eight years this time."

As I climbed the stairs, I thought of embroidery and my desire to learn it. I remembered asking Mother to teach me. But she had put the lessons in the future, beyond my reach—just as Father had. "After the chores are finished," she had told me. "Soon," he had said. I worried that my entire life might be spent waiting for things that would never happen.

Eight

By Monday morning, the warming temperatures escalated to such a point, Uncle Ash officially proclaimed the season Indian summer. I wore my lightest new dress to school that day, without a cloak.

Aunt Sarah handed me an envelope as I was going out the door. "It's an invitation," she said. "Your Uncle Ash wants to meet William. I've asked him to join us and a few of our friends tomorrow evening for tea and dessert."

William was seated at his desk when I reached the classroom. I gave him the invitation. "For you," I said. "It's from my Aunt Sarah."

"What is it?" He examined the envelope from all angles.

"Open it." I watched as he broke the envelope's wax seal and removed a sheet of folded paper, which he opened and read.

He continued to stare at the paper for several seconds before saying anything. "Please tell your aunt that I accept her kind invitation with great pleasure," he said at last.

I returned to my seat, feeling a strange mix of emotions—ranging from excitement and delight to an uneasy foreboding ... a sense that something disagreeable was about to happen.

Tuesday's supper was of no interest to me. I felt fluttery inside, waiting for the festivities to begin. I'd never been to a party before—at least not one that included people from outside our family.

The heat of the day remained in the evening air, causing Aunt Sarah to ask if I would rather wear something light and cool instead of my new dress. "We can have another party later, when winter sets in, so you can show it off," she suggested.

But I had thought about my new dress most of the day. I was eager to see what Father would think of it. I also wondered what *William* would think. His approval was important—because he was exactly the kind of man I hoped to marry someday. Someone good and honest, like Father.

"No," I insisted. "I don't want to wait another minute to put it on. It feels like I've waited years already."

Together, we went upstairs to my room. I took off my school dress; then, while I poured water from the pitcher into the bowl on the washstand, Aunt Sarah left the room. She came back at once with a small bar of soap.

"Use this," she said. "It's imported from France."

"Mmmm, it smells so good."

Aunt Sarah taught me the proper way to wash my face—using just my fingertips to lightly massage the lather over my skin. Then she showed me how to rinse off the suds by cupping the water in my hands and leaning forward into it. At home, I'd always used pieces of our worn-out dish towels to scrub away the dirt and dust of the woods.

71

"Use nothing rougher than your own hands," she warned. "You should always take good care of your skin. It has to last a lifetime."

She left the room again and came back with a tin of cream.

"Here," she said, handing it to me. "Put a dot of this on your cheeks and forehead, and maybe your chin. Just a dot . . ."

I did as she said.

"Good. Now rub it in, but do it gently. Don't stretch your skin. You want it to stay nice and firm."

"Why? So I'll be a beautiful corpse at ninety?"

Aunt Sarah laughed. "Yes, and every day leading up to then."

I hoped that she would disappear again, this time to fetch a pot of rogue and a box of powder. But I supposed that it was just as well she didn't. Father would have made me wash it off before the guests arrived.

Aunt Sarah helped me into my new dress, lifting it over my head and holding out the sleeves so that I could slip my arms through. When I had tried on the dress in Mrs. Sanford's shop, I hadn't bothered with the row of buttons that ran from the base of my neck to the small of my back. I simply held the fabric closed with my hand. But now Aunt Sarah fastened each button—and as she did, I saw that the top was even more formfitting than I had thought at first. I'd never seen my waist so well defined before or the outline of my breasts so obvious.

I studied my reflection in the mirror, wondering if I dared to go downstairs looking that way. But Aunt Sarah chased away my doubts when she said, "You look wonderful."

I noticed that her eyes were moist.

72

"What's wrong?" I asked.

"It's nothing, really. I was just wishing . . ." her voice broke off.

"Wishing what?"

"That your mother could see you tonight."

Because Mary was busy with the refreshments, Aunt Sarah and Uncle Ash stood at the door, welcoming the guests as they arrived. I stood beside them, receiving introductions to each pair of newcomers: Mr. and Mrs. Monroe (he owns the boot shop) . . . Mr. and Mrs. Lewiston (he owns the mill) . . . and Mr. and Mrs. Stoppard (he owns the dry goods store)—all customers of Uncle Ash's bank. Reverend Hunt came alone (his wife was taken by the cholera, not during the most recent epidemic, but during the one two years earlier). By eight o'clock, only two people were missing: William and Father.

I understood Father's reluctance to come downstairs. He didn't have a decent suit of clothes to wear, and he worried that his manners might be too rustic for genteel company. But I felt equally unaccustomed to these new waters. I wanted him beside me for support. I also wanted him to see my new dress, but he hadn't ventured from his room since he went up there after supper.

As Mary was passing the dessert tray for the second time, William finally arrived. I was near the door when he knocked and felt more than willing to extricate myself from Reverend Hunt long enough to let William in. I hurried out into the hallway to the door.

His eyes opened perceptibly wider when he saw me. "Rebecca, you look lovely," he said, emphasizing the last word.

I felt just as I had when he gave me an A+ on a recitation.

"Thank you," I said, then I added, whispering, "I thought you weren't coming."

He whispered back that he had thought the same thing for a while. "There was business that needed my attention," he explained.

"What business?"

"*My* business, not yours," he said, but his voice was kind and his eyes were twinkling.

Aunt Sarah appeared in the parlor doorway. "Mr. Root," she said, extending her hand. "How good to see you."

"The pleasure is mine, I assure you," he said, bowing slightly. His manners appeared practiced, more acquired than natural. I sensed that he would have preferred to be anywhere but there. He made me think of Father. Both were men of very little polish but a great deal of gleam. I realized again that if I were ever to marry, I would want my husband to be as much like them as possible.

Aunt Sarah called out, "Attention, everyone!" She pulled William into the room. "I want to introduce you to my friend—Rebecca's instructor, Mr. William Root."

Uncle Ash went around the room, announcing the names of all the others as he stopped beside them.

"And I," he said, "am Rebecca's Uncle Ash."

William stepped forward to shake hands with my uncle. Just then, Mary came in from the kitchen and I was certain that I saw their eyes meet . . . certain there had been a split second of recognition. But William recovered his poise at once and followed through smoothly with the handshake.

74

I didn't know what to say to my aunt and uncle's friends. I'd never been taught the art of party chatter. It was with relief that I noticed the tea service that had been set up on a table in a far corner of the parlor. I felt a need for something to hold onto and decided that even a delicate china cup would help. I made my way to the table, unaware that Reverend Hunt was following me.

When I finally saw him, it was too late to escape. Because I was in the midst of pouring a cup of tea, I couldn't simply walk away as if I hadn't noticed that he was approaching. He immediately embarked on what seemed to be (at least to him) an urgent topic: my conversion to his religion.

"Our church needs young people like you," he said, "to ensure its future."

Before I could respond, he leaned forward to share a confidence. "That fellow, William Root—is he a good teacher?"

"Why yes, yes he is," I said, surprised by the question.

"I've heard that he's an abolitionist."

"Really?"

"I don't believe it though, do you?" he asked. But it was clear from his tone that he did, indeed, believe it.

"Let's ask him if it's true," I said, moving slightly in William's direction.

Aghast, Reverend Hunt whispered, "Oh no! You can't just *ask* a man something like that."

"But you asked me."

"Well, yes. But it isn't the same."

Reverend Hunt seemed grateful when Mrs. Lewiston joined us. And so was I because he turned his attention entirely to her. That allowed me to slip away, unnoticed, to the other side of the room.

Mr. Monroe and Mr. Stoppard were telling Uncle Ash about some trouble there had been the night before. "Sheriff Bird went from barn to barn all the way down our road," Mr. Monroe said, "looking for another runaway. He said it was a young one this time, a boy about fourteen."

"I hope they caught him," Uncle Ash said.

"Not last night. He got clean away, into Michigan they said. The damned abolitionists took him to catch a boat up by Detroit."

"That's right," Mr. Stoppard added. "All that boat traffic on the river—I used to take it as a sign that business was good, but now I see there's no telling what the cargo might be."

Mr. Monroe chuckled. "A boatload of darkies and abolitionists. Wouldn't we hate to see that one sink?"

All three men laughed hard at that.

"But they finally caught the boy this morning," Mr. Monroe said. "They got him before he made it to the boat. There's no hide nor hair of the scoundrels who helped transport him as far as Michigan, but a U.S. marshal picked up the boy all right—out of a clump of bushes where he was trying to hide."

"The marshal brought him as far as the Wayfarer Inn on Main Street. They've got him all chained up in a room there, waiting for his owner to come and get him," Mr. Stoppard said. "I saw Sheriff Bird when I was on my way here tonight. He said that's one boy who'll be back pickin' cotton tomorrow."

By then, everyone in the room was listening to the

trio of men. I noticed that William was standing by the mantel, watching them in silence. Mr. Monroe edged his way over toward William until he was close enough to speak to him privately, but the level of his voice could easily be heard across the room. "Do they have this much trouble with runaways where you come from, Mr. Root?" he asked.

William smiled slowly before he answered. The room was so quiet, I suspected that all of us were holding our breath. "I wouldn't know, Mr. Monroe," he said. "I don't suppose that runaways generally announce themselves when they go through a town."

"Quite so," Mr. Monroe said. "But still I thought you might know how heavy the traffic was." He looked away from William, toward Mr. Stoppard and Uncle Ash, and gave them a wink. Nervous titters rippled through the room.

Aunt Sarah broke the tension by announcing that a new tray of pastries had just come out of the oven. "Now don't you hurt our Mary's feelings," she said. "Make sure you don't leave a single crumb."

Mary navigated the maze of guests, pausing at each one to offer her array of tempting treats. When she stopped in front of William, she nodded slightly as if in affirmation. It was as quick as a heartbeat, but even so I knew that it was a sign, a communication that the two of them understood. As Mary moved on to the next guest, William lifted a delicate cookie to his mouth—a gesture of pure innocence.

That was all that happened. Nothing more. But that tiny nod of Mary's head had changed William visibly.

For the first time since his arrival, he looked relaxed. Or was it relieved? I couldn't be sure. All I knew was that it seemed as if a great worry, a heavy concern, had been lifted from his shoulders.

Nine

After the last of the guests had left, I went up to Father's room and tapped on the door. He didn't answer, but I went in anyway—and found him asleep. I knew that he planned to leave again early in the morning, so I didn't disturb him. I backed noiselessly out of the room and shut the door.

Just then Aunt Sarah appeared at the top of the steps. "Did you show your father your new dress?"

"I wanted to, but he's asleep."

"Well, he'll just have to wait 'til the next party to see it," she said. "That's what he gets for being so unsociable."

I kissed her good night and went into my room to get ready for bed.

Long after my lamp was out, I lay awake in the dark, unable to sleep. I kept thinking about the party, the things that were said, and the things that were unsaid. I kept remembering the silent communication that seemed to flow between Mary and William. He had said that his arrival was delayed by business that required his attention. I wondered what that business was, and did Mary know about it? And there was something else that bothered me about William. He had arrived dressed for a party. His suit was neat and pressed. His shoes were shined. His hair was combed. But his hands were somewhat dirty. Not filthy, but dirty nonetheless. Whatever it was that he had been doing before his arrival had clearly left its mark.

As I lay awake, too confused to sleep, I thought that I might have heard a sound outside my door. But when I listened more closely, all I heard was silence—until a minute later, when I was certain that I heard movement outdoors beneath my window. I had opened it to let in the delicious night air, one of the last warm nights we could expect before winter set in for good.

I went to the window and looked out but saw nothing. I returned to my bed, but then I heard another noise, something subtle—like footfalls on the path beside the house. Someone lithe. A woman, perhaps. I went back to the window to look down at the path. I saw someone, just a shadow at first, but then he stepped into the moonlight and I saw that it was Father. It was the stealth of a trained hunter that enabled him to step so lightly, but the crunch of dry autumn twigs underfoot gave him away.

I thought that he must be leaving earlier than he had expected, probably because he felt too confined in a fancy house like Aunt Sarah's. But he didn't walk toward the barn where his horse and wagon were. Instead, he veered off, taking the path that led into my uncle's meadow. I watched as he receded into the darkness and disappeared.

Father was not at breakfast when I came down in the morning, but I remembered having seen his belongings when I passed by the open doorway to his room.

"Where's Father?" I asked, settling into my chair at the table. I tried to sound nonchalant, but curiosity had me firmly in its grip. I couldn't imagine where my father might have gone in the middle of the night.

"Still sleeping, I suppose," Uncle Ash said between sips of coffee.

"No. His door is open and his bed is empty."

"Then he's left," Aunt Sarah said.

"No. He wouldn't have left without his leather satchel," I said.

Mary brought us a platter of flapjacks. Aunt Sarah asked her if she had seen Father that morning.

"No, mum," she answered, but there was something about her manner that disturbed me. She appeared more guilty than timid, and that was unlike her. I looked her straight in the eye, but she turned away, flustered.

After Mary left the room, Aunt Sarah remarked that someone ought to teach her some confidence.

"There's no one better than you to do that, my dear," Uncle Ash told her.

"Goodness knows I've tried, but she has no gumption."

Gumption enough to avoid work by pretending to be sick, I thought, remembering how oddly she had behaved when I brought the food to her door. I felt certain that she had been blocking my view. I wondered if there might have been someone in her room . . . someone she didn't want me to see.

We were nearly finished with our meal when there was a knock at the front door. Uncle Ash went to answer it. Several minutes passed before he returned.

When she saw his troubled face, Aunt Sarah asked, "What is it?"

"A bit of trouble," he said. "That was Sheriff Bird."

"Oh?"

A lump of fear caught in my throat. "It isn't Father, is it? He's not hurt, is he?" I asked, forgetting how to breathe.

Uncle Ash touched my shoulder. "Now don't you worry, honey. Nothing's happened to your daddy. Sheriff Bird just wanted to talk to me about the slave boy that Henry Monroe mentioned to us last night."

"The one who's chained up at the hotel?" I asked.

"Well, yes and no. The one who *was* chained up at the hotel. Seems he escaped during the night. He had help, of course. Someone with a ladder, because they found one leaning against the back of the hotel. Standing right up to the boy's room, it was."

An image flashed in my mind: William's hands. I remembered again how they had looked the previous night—somewhat soiled. It was the same look that Father's hands sometimes had after he'd been working in the barn or using his gardening tools.

"Was the ladder dirty?" I asked, but Aunt Sarah and Uncle Ash ignored me, too caught up in their own conversation.

"Sheriff Bird says the boy came this way," Uncle Ash said.

"Why would he think that?" my aunt asked.

"Because the hounds tracked him. They got as far as our place, then lost the scent."

82

Aunt Sarah was all aflutter. "Oh Ash, what if he's in our house?"

"It's much more likely that this is where his helpers took care of confusing the dogs."

"What do you mean?"

"One person goes east with his shirt, another goes west with his stockings—and the hounds don't know which way to go, so they stop."

I laughed, but Uncle Ash's glance quickly silenced me.

I gathered up my books and started out the door to school just in time to meet Father on the porch. He was carrying his rifle.

"Where have you been?" I asked.

"At the cabin. I thought I'd take a look at Victoria and see how they're treating her."

"You went on foot?"

"Well, yes."

"You missed the excitement. Sheriff Bird was here."

A cloud of concern swept over Father's face. "Why? What would bring him here?"

"At first, I thought that something had happened to you, but he had come about a slave boy who escaped."

"I still don't understand. Why would he come here?"

"Because this is where the hounds lost the boy's scent."

"I see," Father said. "And why did you think that something had happened to me?"

"I saw you leave last night."

His surprise was obvious. "You did?"

"Yes, and when you weren't here this morning, and the sheriff came, well . . . I . . ."

He pulled me into a hug. "As you can see, I'm perfectly fine."

"How was Victoria?"

"Hmmm?"

"Victoria. How was Victoria?"

"Oh, yes. Victoria. She was fine."

I pulled back, away from his embrace, so that I could look directly into his eyes. "You didn't really go back home last night, did you?"

Father wrapped his big arms around me again. But he didn't answer me, and that was answer enough. I didn't know the reason, but I did know that my father had lied to me. I thought back to Sunday when Father had said that he was going to take the pelts over to the man who usually bought them. I was as sure as I could be that there had been no pelts in the wagon. It hurt me to think that he would lie like that. His honesty had always been one of the things that I loved most about him.

Something was amiss at school. I felt it even before I knew it, but I couldn't identify why the atmosphere felt so changed, so foreign. Students, many of them assigned to William's class, were divided into several groups of two or three, standing outside the building, talking, when I arrived—and they greeted me in the same warm way they usually did. But when I stepped inside, the air felt oppressive. As I passed by Mr. Halcomb's office, I noticed that the door was open, and, although I couldn't distinguish the words, I did hear voices emerging from the room. I continued toward my class, climbing the steep steps to the third floor. Some of the others were already in their seats when I entered the room, and William was in his usual early morning spot—at his desk. But something was wrong. I could feel it.

The room began to fill up and was nearly full by the time the final bell rang. But only nearly. Margaret Bird's seat was empty.

William had just told us to open our history books to the chapter on the War of 1812 when I heard foot traffic out in the hallway. I turned to see what was happening. Mr. Halcomb entered the room first, moving brusquely toward William. And right at his heels, I saw Mrs. Bird and Margaret. No one was smiling.

I caught Margaret's attention, but she looked away without reading the silent hello my lips had formed. Mr. Halcomb, Mrs. Bird, and William spoke in hushed tones that I couldn't decipher. Margaret went to her desk and took out her books and papers, then the three of them—Mr. Halcomb, Mrs. Bird, and Margaret—left the room.

William followed behind them as far as the door, which he pulled closed before returning to the front of the class.

He cleared his throat, then, in a quiet but steady voice, he announced, "I am sorry to have to tell you that Margaret Bird has decided to attend Reverend Hunt's Christian School."

Aunt Sarah met me at the front door when I came in from school.

"I have a wonderful surprise for you," she said, beaming at me with excitement in her eyes.

She took me by the arm and propelled me into the parlor where Mary stood silent as a statue. But she pulled me past Mary to the love seat. "You have to sit down," she said. "And you, too, Mary."

Mary started toward the rocker by the window.

"No, no, no!" Aunt Sarah said. "Over here, Mary—beside Rebecca."

When we were comfortably settled side by side, Aunt Sarah looked at us for a moment, smiling, as if admiring the arrangement. "Now guess what," she said to me, almost breathless.

I hadn't the slightest notion what I was to guess. Nor did I feel equipped for the game. My mind was too full of thoughts of Margaret Bird. All I wanted to do was to go over to her house and talk to her.

"Guess!" Aunt Sarah said again.

I shook my head, not saying no, but indicating that I had no hypothesis to offer.

"Oh, it doesn't matter," Aunt Sarah. "I'll tell you anyway."

She disappeared into the dining room then returned immediately holding something outward with both hands. "Look!" she said.

I didn't understand. What I took from her was a piece of linen on which there lay several skeins of colored thread, three needles stuck in paper, some small scissors, and an embroidery hoop.

"Well? Aren't you going to say anything?" Aunt Sarah asked.

"Of course . . . thank you . . . I . . . um, love it. Thank you." I knew that Aunt Sarah's mind was a bit scattered at times, but I didn't think she would forget such a recent conversation—the one in which I had asked her to teach me the art of embroidery. She knew that I'd never learned needlework, she knew it plain and simple. I didn't know what to make of her gift.

"And that's not all," she said, still excited. "I am also giving Mary to you—for an hour a day."

I looked at Mary, but her face was impassive.

"I've just found out that Mary is an *expert* with embroidery floss. She has agreed to instruct you for an hour every day."

I stood to give Aunt Sarah a hug. "Thank you, Aunt Sarah. This is the best surprise I've ever received," I said, thinking that now I had two gifts which I had no idea how to use. First, a harmonica. And then all the tools of embroidery, including a teacher who was afraid to say a whole word to me. It wasn't that I was ungrateful. I was delighted to have both. But having them and not knowing how to use them was somehow worse than not having them at all.

I asked Mary when my first lesson would be.

"This very minute," Aunt Sarah said. "I'll leave you girls alone to get started."

I waited until Aunt Sarah was well out of the room before I said, "You don't have to do this, Mary—not if you don't want to."

"Miss Sarah wants me to, miss."

"My name is Rebecca."

"Yes, miss."

"Rebecca," I repeated, then I saw something that I'd never seen before—Mary's smile. It was unexpectedly pretty.

"Rebecca, then," she said.

I sat down beside her to learn how to separate embroidery threads from the skein, and how to place the linen securely in the hoop.

"We'll begin with a cross-stitch," Mary said. "I'll show you how, then you can try it. All you have to remember is to keep the crosses regular in shape and size . . . and always cross the stitches in the same direction."

I was amazed. Mary was capable of saying entire sentences, and, when treated like a person with something to offer, she *acted* like one—drawing confidence and authority from a store that I didn't know she had until then.

We'd been working at the stitches for quite a while, longer than the hour allotted me, when I heard Uncle Ash coming in from outdoors.

At the sound of his boots in the hall, Mary reverted to her skittish self. "Oh dear," she said, "supper! I haven't cooked supper."

She stood, letting the sewing tools fall from her lap. "I'm sorry, miss," she said, stooping to pick them up. As suddenly as that, I was no longer Rebecca, the student, but *miss,* the taskmaster.

Mary moved swiftly out of the room just as Uncle Ash came in, meeting him in the doorway, but he took no notice of her.

"Hello," I said, smiling.

Uncle Ash nodded and tried to return the smile, but his face wouldn't cooperate. He moved closer to take a look at the stitches on the linen, then, seeing that it was woman's work, turned and walked back toward the hallway. He had taken only a few steps when he stopped, faced me, and said, "I saw Tim Dreier today. He came by the bank."

"Tim Dreier? Why do I know that name?"

"He's the fellow who buys most of your father's pelts."

"Yes," I said. "Mr. Dreier. I remember him."

Uncle Ash rubbed his chin. "He said the most peculiar thing to me."

I gave Uncle Ash my full attention.

"He said that he saw your father on the far side of my meadow this morning—before six o'clock."

I didn't find that so peculiar. I knew that Father had left in the middle of the night on mysterious business that he chose not to explain, but it was hardly astonishing for a man to be seen out and about early in the morning.

"Mr. Dreier also said that your father wasn't alone."

"Oh?"

"He said that he was with that teacher of yours— what's his name? Root, isn't it?"

"Yes. William Root," I said, working hard to steady my voice. I felt as if someone had run head-first into my windpipe. A ladder . . . dirty hands . . . a slave boy slipping through the sheriff's fingers . . . lies from my father's lips . . . Father and William in the meadow, *together,* at first light. I couldn't believe it, yet I couldn't disbelieve it, either. Father and William were up to something, and I was afraid that I knew exactly what it was.

"I think Tim Dreier is wrong about that. Your father and your teacher, two men who don't even know each other, being out in my meadow—together— before breakfast?" Uncle Ash said, shaking his head. "Doesn't make any sense."

"No," I said. "It doesn't. Did you tell Mr. Dreier that he was mistaken?"

"Well, now how am I going to do that? I can't tell a man he didn't see what he says he saw."

"But he *is* mistaken. We know that. And even if it were true, what difference would it make?"

"That's the other thing Tim Dreier said today. He said there's a rumor that your father and this Root fellow are in cahoots."

"Cahoots?" I said.

"He told me they're abolitionists. Working together. Your father and Root. What do you make of that?"

"I make nothing of it. It's nonsense," I said, hoping that my face didn't belie my statement.

"Of course it is. That's what I told Tim Dreier. And he said he hoped that I was right, for *my* sake. Abolitionists are bad for business, he said."

"What does that mean?"

"It means that Tim Dreier doesn't plan to put his money in a bank where the owner hobnobs with thieves."

"Thieves?"

"Thieves. Abolitionists. Men who steal another man's property."

"I see," I said.

Uncle Ash sniffed the air. "Smell that? Mary's frying fish for supper. There's no better fish fryer in the whole world than our little Mary, let me tell you."

The memory of the taste seemed to take his mind far away from Tim Dreier and Father. "Your aunt won't let me come to the table with hands like these. I've been handling money all day long—filthy old currency," he said, laughing, but it was clear from his tone that he loved money, worshiped it, filth and all.

He had gotten as far as the archway that leads to the hall when he turned and took a step back toward me. "Uh, Rebecca . . ."

I looked up at him. "Yes?"

"Where did your father say he was this morning when you were looking for him?"

"Why, Uncle Ash," I said with just the hint of a

smile, "I thought you knew. He was out in your meadow with Mr. Root."

Uncle Ash disappeared into the hallway, leaving a trail of laughter behind him.

Ten

My embroidery lesson with Mary and the conversation with Uncle Ash had demanded my attention so fully, I'd nearly forgotten about Margaret Bird. But by the time dinner was over, the feelings from the morning had come flooding back, reminding me how empty I had felt watching my very best friend leaving our classroom.

"Would you mind if I went for a walk?" I asked Aunt Sarah.

"Well, I don't know. Where do you want to go?"

"To Margaret's house. She transferred to Revenend Hunt's Christian School today . . ."

"Oh, dear."

". . . and I didn't have a chance to tell her good-bye."

Aunt Sarah glanced quickly at Uncle Ash, and seeing no protest on his part, she said, "I suppose it would be all right. But I want you back home before it's time to light the lamps, child."

I brushed her perfumed cheek with a kiss and hurried to get my cape.

Margaret's house loomed large and forbidding as I approached the front porch. I swallowed hard before climbing the steps and knocking on the tall wooden door. When no one responded for what seemed like several minutes, I rang the bell. I had been hoping that I wouldn't have to make so much noise. I felt that the less I did to annoy Mrs. Bird, the better. The woman didn't seem to like me much.

I was relieved when Sheriff Bird opened the door. I hadn't been looking forward to having a conversation with Margaret's mother.

"Hello," I said. "I'm ..."

"I know who you are," he told me.

That was the first that I knew he could be as unpleasant as his wife. He didn't smile, and he certainly didn't invite me in.

"May I speak to Margaret for a moment, please?" I asked.

"Margaret isn't here."

"Oh."

Sheriff Bird had the door halfway closed when I asked, "Do you know when she will be here, sir?"

"No."

"Please tell her that I was here," I said, but I said it to a closed door. For several seconds, I stared at the door, trying to figure out what I had done to make Margaret's family dislike me so much. I was still standing there when I heard a sound.

"Pssst!"

I turned toward the side of the house and saw Margaret standing there, half-hidden by some bushes. "Meet me at the cemetery," she called out in a hoarse whisper.

I was glad that the sun was still bright enough to take most of the worry out of walking among the tombstones. I arrived just a minute or two before

Margaret did. Before speaking, she looked back over her shoulder to see if she had been followed.

"I'm so happy to see you," she said. "Mother wouldn't let me say a word to you at school this morning."

"Why did your parents take you out of William's class? Was it because he is an abolitionist?"

"That's part of it," she said.

"Well, what's the rest of it?"

Margaret looked away.

"Is it me?" I asked. "Don't your parents approve of me?

"Oh no, it isn't that."

"What then?"

"It's your father."

Had I been a cat, the fur on my back would have been standing straight up. "What about my father?"

"Well, they say that he's an abolitionist, too. My father told me that your father helped that slave boy escape last night. Your father and William."

I was well aware that I was speaking to the daughter of the town's sheriff. I chose my words carefully so that my visits with Father would not, from then on, be conducted in a jail cell. "My father would never do anything that is wrong."

Margaret reached out and touched my arm. "Don't you see, Rebecca? That's the whole trouble. The people doing those things don't think it's wrong. They think they're doing what's right and good."

I wanted to say "They're right!"—but I knew that I could say nothing that would put my father's welfare in jeopardy.

"And you know what?" Margaret continued. "I'm not so sure they *are* doing wrong."

It took a moment for me to grasp what she had

said. Finally I was able to respond, but only with one meaningless word: "Really?"

"No, no," she said, "I don't mean that. Of course they're doing wrong."

I suppose it was the delay in my response that caused her to take it all back. She was protecting herself from me, just as I was protecting Father from her. I felt better knowing that my friend and I were not so far apart in our feelings as it had, at first, seemed. But I hated not being able to tell her so.

"I'd better get back home," Margaret said. "Before someone misses me."

"Me, too."

We looked at each other, awkwardly, for a moment—then fell into a tearful embrace before saying good-bye.

Eleven

I was jolted awake by someone's hand on my cheek. As soon as I opened my eyes, I saw that the intruder was Mary. Her hand moved quickly to cover my mouth.

"Shhhh . . ."

When she was certain that I was calm, she whispered, "You have to come with me."

"Where?"

"Please. Come with me."

"But I don't understand. What do you want?"

"Please."

The urgency in her eyes told me that I had no choice. I got up, slipped my feet into a pair of slippers, and reached for my robe. I put it on as I followed Mary out the door, into the hall. We progressed slowly, taking care to be as quiet as possible. When we reached the downstairs hall, Mary continued toward the rear of the house, to the back door. But as she reached to open it, I put my hand on her arm, stopping her.

"Where are we going?" I asked, still whispering. "I'm not taking another step until you tell me where we're going."

"To my room ... hurry," she said.

I held back, hesitating.

She took my hand and led me out into the warm, dark night. A light shone through the window of her room, but it was filtered by the curtains, which were closed. She pushed open her door and hurried in, still pulling me by the hand.

What I saw when I stepped inside both shocked and bewildered me. There, in that tiny space, were crowded six people, counting me. The other five were Mary, William, and a family of Negroes—a man, woman, and infant.

"We need your help," William said.

I was confused. I wondered if I might be dreaming.

"This is Timbra," William told me, touching the woman's shoulder. "And her baby, Hosiah."

The Negro man stepped forward and offered me his hand. "I'm Sam. And I'm mighty grateful, miss."

I shook his hand, but couldn't imagine why he felt gratitude toward me.

"Here, put this on," Mary said. She handed me one of the faded cotton dresses she wore while doing Aunt Sarah's housework.

I looked around me, searching for a private place where I could change my clothes.

"Just put it on over your nightgown," Mary said. "Hurry."

I took off my robe, then did as she suggested.

"We have to leave," Mary said. She motioned for the Negroes to follow her as she hurried toward the door. Before going outside, Mary turned to William and said, "Don't forget the loaf of bread."

And then they were gone, leaving William and me alone.

"Will you please tell me what is happening?" I asked.

"Timbra and Sam were going to be separated—taken away from each other and sold. And they didn't know what was to happen to their baby. We are helping them get to Canada."

"When? How?"

"They're going tonight. And you're going to help them get there . . . that is, if you're willing to help us."

I didn't have to give it a thought. "No" was not in my vocabulary that night. "Yes, of course I will."

"Good. In a few minutes one of our people will drive by your uncle's house in a carriage that's pulled by a team of white horses. That's all he will do . . . just ride by. We are to watch for him."

"But why did Mary have me put on this dress?"

"Because you are going to be Timbra tonight, and I am going to be Sam. Mary is taking them overland into Michigan where they will be met by others who will help them board a boat for Canada. And while she does that, you are I are going to lead the sheriff and his deputies toward the river. We want them to think that Timbra and Sam have a boat waiting for them right here because each minute that we can keep them away from Michigan will put Timbra and Sam one minute closer to freedom."

"Why would the sheriff follow us? He's looking for Negroes."

William smiled. "And so we shall be Negroes," he said.

He went to a shelf and took down the unlighted lamp that was sitting there. He ran his fingers down into a soot-covered glass chimney. Then he put one hand under my chin, and lifted my face so that I was looking up into his eyes.

"I'll just put a little of this right here," he said, massaging some of the soot into my cheek. "And here . . . and here . . . and here," he continued, touching my other cheek, my forehead, and my nose.

"You don't need much color," he said. "You're very dark already."

I remembered what Aunt Sarah had said to me that day at the dress shop. I was curious to see how convincing I looked as a slave, but Mary had no mirror.

William took more soot from the chimney and stroked it over the backs of my hands. "Perfect!" he said when he was finished.

"But I *won't* be if I keep perspiring like this," I told him. "All the color will be washed away."

"I'll fix that."

William turned down the wick on the one lamp that was lighted until the flame went out and the room was dark. Then he opened the curtains and pushed up the window, but it wouldn't stay. He looked around for something he could use as a prop to keep it open.

I reached for my robe and pulled my harmonica from the pocket. "Try this," I said.

He pushed up the window again and slid the harmonica into place. But even the open window provided no relief from the heat. I was still sweltering under my double layer of clothing—one of which was a flannel nightgown.

"We need to put something over your hair, too," William said.

He went to Mary's small bureau and opened the top drawer. Because he had no light except that which the moon provided, it took a bit of digging—

but soon he found a paisley shawl. "Here, I think this will work," he said.

He took a knife from his pocket and cut the shawl into two triangles. One he handed to me so that I could wrap it, turban-style, around my head. The other he spread out on the table. He picked up a loaf of bread that was sitting there, placed it in the center of the triangle, and wrapped the cloth around it. When he was finished, he held out the bundle toward me, saying, "This is Hosiah—your baby."

I laughed. "Now what about you?"

William pointed to a small tin on the table. "Burned cork," he said. He handed the tin to me, asking if I would rub the pigment on his face and on the backs of his hands.

The results were remarkable. His color appeared to be authentic—as nearly Negro as a white man's skin could look.

"Now, here's what we're going to do," William said. "We're going to watch for the wagon and the team of white horses. When it goes by, out on the road, that's our sign that the sheriff and his deputies are on their way. That's when you and I—"

"And our loaf of bread—"

"Yes, all three of us. We'll go out to the road and turn toward the river. But we have to be careful. We have to stay so far ahead of them, they can't possibly catch us—yet we have to remain close enough so they can easily see us."

"But what if they *do* catch us?"

"If you want to back out, Rebecca, now is the time to do it."

"I don't want to back out. I just want to know what will happen if we're caught."

"I suppose we'll go to jail," he said.

Just when William had taken his post at the window—to watch for the wagon and the white horses—they appeared.

"All right," he said. "This is it."

We moved as silently as we could along the side of the house, heading toward the road. I was thankful that I was wearing my slippers. The soft soles were nearly soundless on the path.

We waited at the edge of the road, concealed behind a huge buckeye tree, watching for the sheriff and his men in the distance.

It was only a minute, no longer, before we saw the glow of the posse's lanterns coming over the rise of the hill.

William whispered, "Run!"—and I did, but not so fast that the searchers would lose sight of me. I was aware of William at my side, keeping pace. Every few seconds he looked back over his shoulder, never once altering his stride. "We're doing fine," he said. "Just fine."

But I wasn't used to running. I didn't know how much farther I could go. We must have covered nearly a mile before I felt the first sharp pain in my throat—a pain that tightened and grew until I could barely breathe.

"I don't think I can keep going," I said.

"You *have* to."

"I can't."

A minute later I had to slow down.

"I'm sorry. I just can't do it. I have to stop."

"You can't stop."

"I have to. I can't help it."

William looked back once more. "We have a good

distance between us. You're doing fine. Just keep it up."

As we were approaching the edge of the woods, the pain shot up to the top of my throat, all the way to the roof of my mouth. I slowed down almost to a walk.

William must have known that it was useless—that I couldn't go on. "I'll lead them off to the left," he said. "The first chance you get, leave the path ... duck into the tall grasses and hide. I'll stay in the moonlight where they can see me."

We ran a few more yards, and then I saw my opportunity—a perfect opening between the trees. As I veered off the path, the sound of William's footfalls moved farther and farther away from me.

I stopped for an instant, trying to catch my breath. The pain in my throat was subsiding some, but I felt too weak and shaky to run. When I moved again, it was at a brisk walk—until I heard voices.

"I think she's over here, on the right," a man said.

I stood totally still—silent, except for the beating of my heart. Then I thought of the bread. I pulled it out of the shawl and threw it as hard and as far as I could, aiming it in the direction of the path that I had just left. It landed several feet away.

"Wait!" another man called out. "She's over there!"

I heard them moving away from me, back toward the path, traveling the same direction the loaf of bread had.

When I could no longer hear them, I inched my way deeper into the woods, moving noiselessly—as Father had taught me to do when hunting. Soon I came to a place that I thought I recognized. And then, when I saw the felled tree lying on the ground, I remembered. It was the same small clearing where Margaret and I had sat on the hollow log and giggled about the mail carrier who had nearly burned up when hiding from wolves.

I heard a noise and knew at once what it was. The men had left the path again, and they were coming through the brush in my direction. I did the only thing I could—I dropped down to the ground and crawled inside the log, just as the mail carrier had done. But it was more difficult than I had expected. The inside of the log was sharp in places, and rough everywhere—tearing at my skin as I scooted myself deep inside. The wrap on my head caught on something and was pulled off, then strands of my hair were the next to go. I moved as far inside as I could before the log narrowed, blocking my progress. I lay motionless, listening and waiting. Trembling and praying.

It felt like a long time, but I know that it couldn't have been, before I heard the men approaching the log.

"I think we've lost her."

"But I was sure she came this way."

"Probably just an animal."

"Well, I think they got the boy."

"Yep. Reuben was right on his tail."

"Yep."

Something was crawling on my nose, but I couldn't brush it away. I was stuck in a position that left my arms paralyzed at my sides.

"How about sitting down for a minute?" one of the men asked.

Someone kicked the log, causing something mushy and wet to fall on my face. "Seems good and solid," a voice said. "Let's sit here."

103

The top of the log sank under the weight of them, pressing on my shoulders.

"Sure is hot for a September night."

"Sure is."

If they thought they were hot out there, they should have tried climbing inside a wet log—wearing two layers of clothing. I wondered if I would ever be able to get out. Going forward had been difficult enough. I couldn't imagine what it would be like trying to move in reverse. The only way to find out if I could do it was to try it, but I couldn't. Not until the sheriff's men left.

"Is there a reward for these slaves we're chasing?"

"There is for the boy. But as far as the woman and the baby, I don't know. I don't think so."

Mrs. Stowe's book had made it clear that women and children weren't as valuable as male slaves. They couldn't handle the really hard work.

"I wonder what gets into these niggers—running away like that. I wonder what they're thinking."

One of them laughed. "Thinking? They don't think. They're just slaves."

They both laughed then.

I felt some movement, a slight rolling sensation when the men stood up.

"Might as well go on back."

"Right. We can wait for Reuben and the others up at the tavern."

I remained still for a long time after the men walked away, worried that maybe it was a ruse—a trick to bring me out of my hiding place. I don't how long it was . . . maybe an hour, maybe more. And the longer I waited, the more nauseated I became from the stench inside the log. It was a mix of mildew and mustiness, rotting vegetation and moldy wood. Even

104

now, I shudder when I think of it. I tried to think of other things—*any*thing but the sickening odor.

But my alternative thoughts weren't much more pleasant. I was worried that I might die inside that log, with no one ever finding me. The smell of my decaying flesh would simply blend with the existing stench. No one would ever suspect that I was there. I wondered what Father would think if I were to disappear that way, leaving no clues.

I thought about Margaret, too. I felt sad that I might never see her again. I also felt sad that I might never learn to play my harmonica. And I felt even worse to think that I might never embroider a sampler. But the worst feeling of all came when I thought of all those squares that Mother had embroidered. That they might remain forever in a box under Father's bed, that they might never be sewn together to form the quilt she had imagined—these thoughts were more than I could bear. Tears spilled out of my eyes, into the raw scratches on my face.

After an hour or maybe more, I decided to risk leaving the log. I found that by adjusting my hips the little bit that I was able to move, and by rocking my weight from side to side, I could creep gradually backward—but the skirts of both my dress and my nightgown inched upward as I moved, exposing my legs to the sharp, protruding surfaces. By the time I had wiggled myself free, I was covered with abrasions, especially on my toes and knees. A strong breeze had begun to stir, and every time it touched the raw places on my skin, I winced in pain.

I hadn't even half an idea of how I would explain my physical damage to Aunt Sarah and Uncle Ash, but that didn't stop me from heading back to the sanctuary of their home.

I passed no one on the road. When I reached the house, I went in by the front door and sneaked up the stairs like a burglar. I made it safely into my room and shut the door.

The water from my pitcher felt harsh on my injuries, but I knew that I had to wash away not just the dirt—but also the smell—of my hiding place. Putrid debris was lodged in my hair. Not even my hairbrush could pry it free. Instead, I had to sit at my dressing table, carefully separating foul flora from each tangled strand. I had nearly finished when, out of the corner of my eye, I noticed movement reflected in my mirror. I turned toward the door and watched as it continued to open. I thought my heart would explode.

Uncle Ash stepped in and closed the door behind him.

"I expect an explanation, young lady," he said. As he came closer, he saw my condition. "What in tarnation happened to you?"

I couldn't think of an answer, except the truth—and I couldn't tell him that. When I didn't respond, he sat down on the bed, letting me know that the matter wouldn't end so easily.

"Something odd happened tonight, Rebecca," he said. "I was in bed, sound asleep, when a strange noise awakened me. It was like a sound from another world—almost like a ghost whining in the night."

"What was it?"

"Well, that's just it, Rebecca. I didn't know. I couldn't imagine. But it kept up. On and on it went. So I got up out of bed and went looking for it, to see what it was. It sounded like it was downstairs, so that's where I went. But as soon as I was down there,

106

I realized that it wasn't there at all . . . it was outside."

He paused, looking at me as if he expected me to say what it was.

"So then I went out back," he said. "And there it was."

He paused again.

"There what was?" I asked.

"The thing that was making that weird noise. And you know what it was?"

I shook my head no.

"It was the wind blowing through a harmonica."

I got goose bumps when he said that.

"That's right," he continued. "A harmonica! It was wedged in under the window in Mary's room, to hold it open. And it wasn't just any harmonica, was it, Rebecca?"

I swallowed hard as he took the harmonica from his pocket and placed it on my lap.

"It was *your* harmonica, wasn't it?"

I looked down, unable to meet his eyes.

"Well, I got to wondering what Mary was doing with your harmonica, so I thought I'd ask her. I knocked on her door—but you know what? She didn't answer. There it was, after midnight, and the girl didn't answer."

I couldn't stop staring at my lap.

"So I got worried about her. I thought I'd better check to make sure that she was all right. I opened the door to her little house and looked inside. And do you know what I saw then?"

I shook my head, still unable to look at him.

"I saw your robe, Rebecca, lying there on a chair. And I asked myself, why would your harmonica and your robe be out there in Mary's room? I was also

107

kind of curious about Mary. I wondered where she might be in the middle of the night. So what do you think I did then?"

I shrugged. For the second time that night, tears crept down my cheeks.

"I came back in the house and went right up to your room—to ask you what you knew about the harmonica and the robe . . . and to see if you knew where Mary might be. And do you know what I discovered?"

"That I wasn't here," I said in a whisper.

"What?" he thundered, making me afraid to say the words again.

"I discovered that your bed was empty—and that *you* were gone, too, just like Mary. I tried and tried, but I couldn't figure out what was happening. So I went out to the front of the house, to the lawn, to see if you girls were out there. You weren't, of course, but do you know who I saw walking by?"

I shook my head.

"I saw some of the sheriff's men. There they were, walking past the house, coming from the direction of the woods. And when they saw me, they asked if I had seen a nigger man or his woman and baby. They said all three of them belong to a man in Kentucky, and they were due to go to auction—but they took off running instead."

The tears were flowing faster by then.

"*You* don't have any idea where they ran, do you, Rebecca?"

I shook my head again.

"Or who they ran with? Maybe it was with someone who put on some of that burned cork that Mary has sitting out there in her room. What do you think about that?"

I buried my face in my hands.

"Looks like you don't have any thoughts on that. So maybe you have some thoughts on this: I was wondering what you think about getting on back to your own home. Real soon."

I looked at him then, but still couldn't speak.

"I was thinking tomorrow would be a good time. Or tonight."

"Please, Uncle Ash," I said at last, "don't do this."

"I can't afford to be harboring abolitionists in my house."

He stood up then and walked toward the door. Before he went out into the hallway, he looked at me one last time and said, "I'll try to think up something to tell Sarah. Why don't you just be on your way before she wakes up in the morning?"

He closed the door behind him.

I ran to my bed and fell facedown into the feather mattress, weeping nearly as hard as I had when Mother died.

Twelve

I was gone well before dawn and left behind all my new dresses, as well as Aunt Sarah's cloak and shoes. I was tempted to take the embroidery supplies but decided not to. I didn't want Uncle Ash to have any further complaints about me.

I put a note at Aunt Sarah's place at the table. *I'm sorry* is all I wrote, except for *Love* and my name.

I was too hurt—emotionally and physically—to feel as afraid as perhaps I should have, going out into the night alone. But I did have enough good sense not to go into the woods until daylight. Instead, I headed toward the center of the town, toward the apothecary shop. I remembered William saying that he lived in the apartment above it, and I wanted to tell him good-bye.

A steep stairway on the side of the building led up to a door that I assumed to be William's. I climbed the stairs and rapped lightly on the pane in the door. I couldn't see any lamplight inside, but after a moment I heard movement. Soon the latch turned and the door opened. A sleepy-eyed William, clad in a nightshirt, squinted through the dark.

"Rebecca? Is that you?" He came awake quickly then. "I was so worried!"

He pulled me into the room and closed the door. Then he lit his lamp and held it close to me. "What happened to you? You're covered with bruises."

I knew how terrible I must have looked. I asked him to please put out the light, but he didn't.

"Have you heard anything about Timbra and her family?" I asked. "Did they make it to the boat?"

"I don't know yet," William said. "We'll probably know in the morning."

"It is morning already," I said.

"Yes, you're right. And you'd better get back to your uncle's house before someone discovers that you're missing."

"I can't go back there. Uncle Ash knows everything. He made me leave."

"Where's your father?"

"Hunting."

"Then you'll stay here," William said. He gestured toward a chair. "Sit down. I'm going to wash off those bruises and put some medicine on them."

I watched as he went about the business of repairing me. Carefully, tenderly, he cleaned the worst of the abrasions on my arms, legs, and face. Then he opened a tin and scooped out some ointment on the tip of his finger. This, he rubbed gently into each sore spot.

"Thank you," I said when he was finished.

"And thank you," he said.

"For what?" I asked.

"For being so brave." He looked closely at me then and asked, "Are those tears? Are you crying?"

"Only a little."

111

He caught one tear with his hand and wiped it away. "What's wrong?"

"I'm so afraid . . . what's going to happen to you?"

Suddenly there was the sound of voices outdoors. "Shhh," I said. "Listen."

William put out the light. We sat in the dark, listening, as the voices drew closer. A moment later we heard footsteps on the stairs, then there was pounding on his door and someone hollering, "William Root, open up! You're under arrest."

"Hurry," William whispered, "crawl under my bed and keep completely quiet. Don't come out until after they have taken me away, or they will take you, too."

As I did as he instructed, the pounding on the door grew louder, more urgent. From my hiding place, I heard the door open and listened as the sheriff and his deputies arrested William.

I stayed in William's apartment until the sun came up. By noon, I was in my own home. Father returned from Fulton County three days later, after stopping first at Aunt Sarah's. He told me that he had parted company with both Aunt Sarah and Uncle Ash. It was firm and final, he said, but not without difficulty. I understood what he meant. I had no sympathy for their views, but I loved them, both of them, with a love that was deep and dear.

"I suppose I'm a fortunate man," Father said. "The bears will continue to do business with me, no matter how many slaves I assist."

I knew, from that comment, that Father made allowances for Uncle Ash. "None of us can be sure what we would do in his position until we are as threatened as he was," he said.

"But no one threatened him."

"You did, Rebecca. You threatened his livelihood just by staying in his house. It takes a big man to ignore such a threat, and behave as you and I would prefer."

"Do you think he will ever change?"

"He may."

"When?"

"When men's attitudes toward abolitionists change."

He might as well have said "Never."

I asked Father why he had lied to me that morning when he told me that he had gone home to check on our cow—when, in fact, he had been helping a slave boy find his way through the swamp at night.

"I didn't want to give you too much responsibility," he said. "It can be a terrible burden."

"What do you mean?"

"If I had told you my secret and you had revealed it to the wrong person by accident, would you ever have forgiven yourself?"

"Not if you were taken to jail," I said, thinking of William.

"You see?" he asked. "I was just protecting you."

What an autumn it had been. I had learned that some kinds of stealing weren't stealing at all. And I had learned that some lies were easier to forgive than others.

Soon after Father returned, word reached us that Timbra, Sam, and their baby had arrived safely in Canada—and William was no longer in jail. He was taken before a justice of the peace, a man secretly involved in the Underground Railroad, who imposed a hefty fine. It was immediately paid by another abolitionist who had passed the hat among his friends. But

William did lose his teaching position at the high school. I heard that he went back East.

Tonight I pulled the box out from under Father's bed and removed the embroidered squares. I spread them out on the floor, trying to decide how Mother would have arranged them. Because I am a person who works best within a structure, I began by arranging them alphabetically—azaleas, buttercups, cornflowers—but I soon realized that would not have been my mother's way of doing it. She was an artist, more susceptible to the harmony of colors than the sequence of letters. I began again.

Father had been chopping wood outside the door. When he came in, he saw what I was doing.

"What's this?" he asked.

"Mother's needlework. She meant to make a quilt, and I want to finish it."

He stood slightly behind me, watching, for some time. Then he sat down on the floor beside me and picked up one of the squares. "My favorite shirt," he said, looking at the piece of fabric as if it were a priceless treasure.

"And your favorite flower."

He nodded. "Yes, Queen Anne's lace. How did she know?"

"She probably watched you. You never passed by the bush when it was in bloom without stopping to touch it."

"What about this one?" he asked. He was holding a square of calico.

"Lily of the valley."

"No, I mean the fabric."

"It's from that dress I wore when I won my first spelling bee."

114

He smiled. "Yes, yes," he said, enjoying the memory.

It went on like that for many hours—both of us touching the fabric that Mother had touched, trying to remember what she had remembered as she worked. And so it was that we constructed a history that, when glimpsed whole, revealed a garden that was uniquely ours—Father's, Mother's, and mine. The memories were ours to pluck, one at a time, like flowers—or to bundle in glorious bouquets. That night, it seemed as if we had put on magic spectacles that changed our view of the past, diminishing our hours of heartache, enlarging our moments of joy. And what we saw when we looked ahead to the future was a chance to expand our garden. I knew then that if we planted the seeds, they would grow into memories as beautiful as those that Mother had embroidered for us.

Since then, there have been many nights when, if the wind is still and the crickets are asleep, I am almost certain that I can hear a sweet song—merry and melodious—echoing in the grove.

PATRICIA SIERRA lives with her two cats, Ki-Ki and Toe-Toe, in Toledo, Ohio—in the heart of one of the neighborhoods that was hardest hit by the cholera epidemic depicted in this book, and just a few miles from the swampy forest where Rebecca, the book's heroine, lived.